January 2004

For my most talented
outdoors (boy) Jenner —

- one who loves the thrill
  of mountains —

- one who respects mother
  nature's whims —

- one who adores the
  adventures life has to
  offer

- one who can plan an
  expedition and follow it
  Through —

- one who appreciates long
  journeys .... perhaps on horse !

Enjoy this old book —

  The older the folklore —
    the better —
  but this is not
  fiction... it is
  For real !

love
your
auntie
Andrea

P.S. Look at The
  photo plates to see
  for yourself before
  you start reading !

JOURNEY
FROM
THE ARCTIC

JOURNEY
FROM
THE ARCTIC

✺

D.C. BROWN

✺

NEW YORK

ALFRED A. KNOPF

1956

L. C. catalog card number: 55–9273

┌─────────────────────────────────────┐
│ THIS IS A BORZOI BOOK,   │
│ PUBLISHED BY ALFRED A. KNOPF, INC. │
└─────────────────────────────────────┘

FIRST AMERICAN EDITION

"*Day after day, week after week, and month after month, your foot is in the stirrup. To taste the cold breath of the earliest morn, and to lead or follow your bright cavalcade till sunset through forests and mountain passes, through valleys and desolate plains—all this becomes your mode of life. . . . If you are wise, you do not look upon the long period of time thus occupied by your journeys as the mere gulfs which divide you from the place to which you are going; but rather, as most rare and beautiful portions of life, from which may come thought, temper and strength. Once feel this, and you will grow happy and contented in your saddle-home.*"

EOTHEN

Preface

"A perfect Englishman—travelling without motive." VOLTAIRE

THERE is no excuse for this journey. It had no scientific purpose, it proved nothing, it collected nothing. The only thing to be said for it is that we enjoyed it and learned a little by it. It was travelling for travelling's sake.

It was a droll journey. I have heard of no expedition so ill-equipped. Hardly anything happened but the unexpected. Almost the only event that was almost serious happened after we had left the Arctic and most of the snow. Most singular of all was the extent to which our absurdly inadequate equipment proved adequate. Certainly a bit more would have meant more comfort (and more trouble), but the fact remains that the journey was completed on our comb-and-toothbrush equipment without disaster. With more we might have escaped a bout of rheumatism (or whatever it was) and been less hungry more often, but that is all.

We chose to go on horseback because we believed that,

from the days of the Crusaders, Genghis Khan, and Marco Polo, this has been the most absorbing and eventful way of travel. And, apart from walking, which can be pedestrian in more senses than one, it is also the most versatile: no one mechanical contraption could have gone over snow, through forests, and crossed becks, marshes, and mountains as the horses did.

On a journey of six months there is more of the daily round than of incident, more of amusement than of adventure. I have tried to keep a reasonable balance between incident and the long pull of the trek. Much the greater part of your time is spent jogging ruminatively along a track, enjoying the taste of your pipe and your freedom from convention and the clock, feeling grateful for a warming sun or grousing at a bitter wind, talking of anything in the world with your companion, listening to an annoying creaking from your saddle, and, most of all, going over the delights of your last meal or wondering when the next one will come. If you live on the country and live for the day, then the most important thing most of the time is your belly. You are more gluttonous than gallant.

Author's Note

IN a book such as this there is certain to be much mention of natural features and place names. In Scandinavia the former are often tacked on to the latter, and to translate is to spoil the harmony of sound as well as being an offence to Scandinavian eyes, just as it would offend ours to read of Evesham-dal or Thameselv or Ullsvatn. A glossary can be tiresome, but I give here a short list of names; those who know the English lakes will have no difficulty, as so many Norse names have survived here. The words *saeter* and *bruk* are used because there is no exact English equivalent.

Swedish or Norwegian	Lake District	Usual English
Fjell	Fell	Mountain
Bekk	Beck	Stream
Vatn	Water	Lake
Foss	Force	Waterfall
Dal	Dale	Valley
Elv, Alv		River

Bruk: Small, primitive farm in forest or mountains
Saeter: Clearing in mountains for pasture

: xi :

CONTENTS

ILLUSTRATIONS

(PHOTOGRAPHS BY THE AUTHOR AND G.S.)

FOLLOWING PAGE 46

FOLLOWING PAGE 142

: XV :

Illustrations

JOURNEY
FROM
THE ARCTIC

1. Genesis

The seed ye sow, another reaps. SHELLEY

BETWEEN the first thought of this journey and its beginning were twelve years and seven thousand miles. Conceived beneath the sun in Africa, it was born in the snow of the North, and meanwhile the world had changed. It had been rather like waiting for the birth of a baby elephant in a travelling circus.

The idea first came to Griff in 1939, in the Transvaal. The day was one for spacious thoughts: the wide yellow veld spread out beneath the sun to a far horizon broken only by *kopjes* vibrating in the hot air and a cluster of native kraals sprouting stems of smoke from bulbous cooking-pots. There was a pleasant, pungent smell of sweating horses and a quiet tinkle of bits; dust rose around us from loitering hoofs and settled on our burning arms.

We had turned to reminiscing. There was the time we took the horses to the beer garden in Johannesburg and they sucked ale from a bucket; the day down in the Karro when Comet, happy little demon, dumped me in the mud of Tarka Dam, whence I spluttered curses at him as he capered and caracoled gleefully upon the bank; the night when we had ridden in evening dress for seven miles to a New Year's hop at the neighbouring dorp and cantered back through the crisp, moonlit night, black silhouettes with flowing tails against the milky sand, like lost shades of highwaymen who had forgotten their haunts; and the hard, peaceful days driving cattle from the Rhodesian ranch down to West Nicholson when mealies and biltong were caviar and sleep was heaven. A long way it was and three long weeks it took us. Those were good days in the sun, and good nights when in your health and tiredness you laid your head in infinite comfort upon the bosom of your saddle and the cool night came down upon your face.

So we fell to thinking of them. The sharing of experience had brought us the understanding that needs no speech, so often we went in long silences without awkwardness or offence. At last Griff said, as though we had spoken all the while: "Yes, those were good days. I wouldn't mind doing a ride like that again, only longer. This is a good country for it." I knew this was no idle talk.

Later, as we rested in the evening stillness a silence came upon us, broken only by plops from peaceful pipes. At last I broke the silence:

"Were you serious about that ride?"

"Yes, of course."

He lay back, clasping hands beneath his head, and spoke slowly and thoughtfully as though to himself.

"The size of a journey is decided by time, not distance. If you want a journey worth the name, you must go on legs— your own, or borrowed ones. The best way is on a horse, because your search for fodder will bring you to the people of the country. In a car or a plane or a ship you travel in a little island of isolation from knowledge or adventure. You can take a car and cross the world's greatest desert in a week—on a road—and sleep under a roof every night. But there's a thousand miles each side of the road where you would have to go on a camel, and that would be a real journey. If you want adventure, you mustn't go too fast for it to catch up with you, nor set out with every invention to increase your comfort. Today expeditions load up with wireless, typewriters, boxes of stores, tents, and vitamin pills. Take nothing invented in the past six hundred years and you can travel as interestingly as Marco Polo. Y'know, the much-spewed 'The world's grown smaller' and 'Adventure is dead' are poppycock. It's imagination that's dead and the mechanization of travel alive and stinking as a pole-cat. There's enough left in the world to feed the most gluttonous of adventurers if he'll look for the right place and go into it and not through or over it."

He groped in the grass for his pipe and lit up the dottle. Then he got up and said: "Oh well, we've a long day tomorrow. I'm off to bed," and strolled to the rondavel, humming quietly to himself.

But the idea was already tacitly accepted. In the uneasy weeks before the war, plans and routes were discussed and made for a start from Cape Town to the north shortly before Christmas, when weather and grazing for the horses would be at their best. Then suddenly war came; I sailed to England and the Army and Griff joined the South African Air Force. "It won't be long before it's over," we said, "and then we can get started." But it was long, and somewhere in Africa is Griff's grave.

During the war the plan was almost forgotten; at its end, perhaps because Griff had seemed an essential part of the journey, it was no more than a dream dug up to brighten moments of monotony in the life of a riding-instructor. But I always believed that some day the journey would come to life, and in the autumn of 1950 that day came.

2. Plans and Preparations

Though this be madness, yet there is method in 't. SHAKESPEARE

IN these cramped days there seems no room for the old-fashioned terrestrial globe. It is a pity, for he was a jolly gentleman, with his Pickwickian paunch showing the world as it is, undistorted by projections and the other complications of trying to make a ball flat, as though it had not enough eccentricities as it is. It gave such importance to a room, as though its owner and the earth worked in the closest co-operation. As a small boy on visits for correction to my housemaster's study I was deeply impressed by his idle dallying with the earth between his fingers, in intimate disregard for its normal speed and direction of rotation on its ornate axis, while he heard my hopeful explanation and considered sentence. Now, alas, it seems that these globes suggest omnipotence only in the shining offices of airlines, who run thick red lines across them as though they had constructed the world specially to fly their planes around.

But what the map lacks in solidity it makes up for in handiness, and its study may be the pleasantest of preparations for a journey. I took out one of the world. There was now no reason to ride in Africa should another part of the world be better, and I traced out the long horseback journeys of which I had read or heard tell. They went through central Asia, India, and Persia, the savanna belts of Africa north of the Equator, southern Europe, and southern Canada. And most classic of them all was Tschiffely's ride from Buenos Aires to Washington. But there seemed no point in following an already trodden path, so I lost myself in a dozen possibilities in adjoining parts of the world. This map was certainly no niggard; indeed, it was embarrassing in its generosity, and its too great choice was almost as bad as none at all. In indecision my eyes wandered upwards to the North. As all these other journeys had been to the south of our latitudes, I had unthinkingly supposed the North to be impractical. It is of course the preserve of travellers by sledge and, on the face of it, not suited to riding on horseback. Three doubts came to mind: was there food for horses, would they stand the cold, and would the snow bear the weight of a ridden horse? (I say snow because to go to the North except in the winter seems scarcely in place or even sporting, like wearing your hat without your trousers or netting salmon.) I remembered that the Russians used horse-drawn sledges, but was that only in towns and villages or upon hardened tracks? The knowledge I had gathered of riding in more southerly latitudes seemed of little use here, and I felt beyond my depth. But the idea interested me by its singularity, and I searched the top of the map methodically, beginning at the west. Alaska and Canada certainly offered plenty of room and there was some fine country of mountains, rivers, and forests, but their tale had been so often told by novel and film, even if a little fancifully. They seemed to have suffered from blarney and to have too little history. And in the southern parts I feared mechanization and the milk bar.

Iceland seemed more interesting. There was, I believed, a sparsely inhabited interior of lava mountains and geysers, and a hardy native pony. But as it is an island and slightly less in area than England, there was little space for a long-distance ride, and being south of the Arctic Circle, it is not truly in the North.

Regretfully I left it and turned to northern Europe: to Lapland, northern Russia, and Siberia. I knew little of Lapland apart from its being the land of Lapps and reindeer. Russia and Siberia had great spaces little known, but a communized people did not offer much colour though they did offer an early end to a vagrant Englishman. So I turned back to Lapland. I knew of no one who had been there, which was good; neither could I remember having read a book or seen a film of it, which was better. It had a colourful people. It was well within the Arctic Circle. Probably there were trails across the snow hardened by reindeer and their sledges. And by going through Finland into northern Sweden I could go as far south as I wished. It seemed that Lapland was what I wanted, but there was a lot to be found out before I could be certain.

The more learnt beforehand of a country's geography, history, people, language, food, and drink, the more interesting it will be to travel in. Lacking some of this knowledge, one may as well sit at home and read a guide-book and look at picture postcards. And if one is finding one's own way in a mercifully undeveloped country, either this knowledge or an extraordinary amount of luck is necessary. One should be foolish wisely. I found out all I could about Lapland from encyclopædias, books on geography, and from the only book I could find on winter travel in this part of the world. Also, I bought one of Bartholomew's excellent contoured maps, which tell more of a country than most books.

I probed the travel agencies. Could they give me any information, any leaflets or maps of Lapland? There came no confident smiles, but disappearance to seek help from a colleague, or a tedious searching through a pile of pamphlets. You felt that perhaps their firm didn't deal with Lapland. One produced a pamphlet of Swedish Lapland, but northern Lapland!—no one went there in the winter. They had heard of someone going in the summer, there was excellent salmon-fishing when the rivers broke up, they believed, and a very good cruise round the North Cape in the Land of the Midnight Sun: perhaps I would like this pamphlet about it? Better to wait till the summer; and they smiled at my eccentricity. Besides, there were no railways, and no roads worth the name and in any case they would be covered in snow. The only way would be by reindeer sledge, so how could I travel? On horseback, I admitted. On horseback? A punch-drunk pause. I became aware of the extreme sanity of polished walls, posters of Eastbourne and Nice, name plates upon the counters, and the efficient clicking of typewriters, and wondered whether after all I was what they thought I was. Desperately they suggested I might get some information from the embassies in London. I thanked them and crept out with my pamphlet of "A Cruise to the Land of the Midnight Sun."

In London I was given the address of one Astri Tonberg, who lived at Bossekop, about thirty miles from Hammerfest on the coast of northern Lapland. I wrote, and received a long and helpful letter in reply. In short, it seemed that— though such a journey in winter had not, so far as was known, been done before and was not considered advisable— there was no reason why it should be impossible.

I searched for some account of a horseback journey over snow so that I might benefit from another's experience. The only one I could find told of the retreat of Napoleon's cavalry from Moscow. This was scarcely either encouraging or satisfactory: not satisfactory because the cases were not parallel, for, though Lapland is between five and eight hundred miles further north than Moscow, it was to be expected that the people would be friendly and that wherever there was food and shelter for horse and rider, it would be available. I finished the story feeling sorry for Napoleon and his men.

Having collected all the information I could, it was now time to plan roughly the route, though details could only be determined on the way and must be collected locally from time to time. Hammerfest, the most northerly town in the world, seemed a logical starting-point; I could take ship there from Bergen in southern Norway. From Hammerfest I could either go down the jagged coast of Norway or go over the Lapland plateau, across the tongue of Finland, into the forests of northern Sweden; then turn westward over the mountains into Norway and down the coast to Trondheim, thence through the Jotunheimen Mountains into the fiord country and to the south. Politically, the Finnish section called for thought. Finland is narrow in the north and thus exposed to Russian influence, and parts of it are occupied by them. It seemed doubtful whether I could get a visa, for at that time they were not always easily obtained for the North. On measuring the map I found that the narrowest point where a crossing could be made was only some thirty miles that might be ridden during the night by a forced stage with horses fresh from a day's rest upon the border, and the chances of meeting a ski patrol in this almost uninhabited region were small. But it was my good fortune that the Finnish Consul to whom I went both for information and a visa was a horseman and a traveller, and interested in my intention. In ten days he gave me both the visa and his best wishes for the journey.

I had the idea of continuing through Europe, keeping carefully to the sunnier side of the Iron Curtain, and so down through Turkey to the Levant. But a strictly enforced travel allowance prevented this (the Treasury was not to be persuaded that one travelled on horseback on a business trip) and, looked at dispassionately, it was perhaps a good thing, for the journey through Europe might have proved a long hiatus in the middle of the ride.

Whether to go on such a journey by yourself or try to get a companion is not easy to decide. Much may be said for either. Travelling alone means more freedom, as you choose your own route and your own times; without need to compromise, you sink deeper into the country, notice more and feel more, for on long, lonely stages your eyes and ears have no competitor but your thoughts. And though you have been so long with your own habits that most of them have ceased to annoy you, God knows how they may affect another.

On the other hand, with a companion you can form your impressions better by exchanging them; you can pile your pet theories and arguments, your grumblings and your attempts at humour upon him so much more satisfactorily than upon an immutable Nature or even the boundless tolerance of your horse. Where one may speak the native language and have a little veterinary knowledge, the other may know best how to build a bivouac and have a flair for talking round frontier officials. On the whole, I think it better to go with a companion, providing he is tolerant enough to endure yourself and the more repellent of your habits, and, above all—and this is essential—that he has a sense of humour. (There is, of course, no doubt that you have one yourself.) Without these two virtues to go with you, you do better alone.

You will not find another easily. You may say to one or

two of your more likely friends and acquaintances: "What fun it would be to go from here to there, by such and such a means." Possibly they will agree; just the sort of thing they'd always wanted; if only they had a chance, they'd be off tomorrow. Encouraged, you ask: "Well, what about it? I've been looking into the best ways of doing it," and you launch off eagerly into details. Probably there will be a dulling of enthusiasm; reasons will be found to prove the journey impossible. If you know your stuff, you can show every one to be false. But at last: "Well, of course, you know, if you'd asked me before this happened, or that, I'd have come. But I can't leave my job," or: "I've got a wife." You are wasting your time. He who is not keen enough to risk losing his job or his wife, or is not confident of getting himself another if he should, is no good to you on a journey. You will then do as I did: go sadly away and advertise.

The correspondence columns of a riding-paper seemed likely to be the most profitable. Five replies came to my letter, one of which, from a Dane in Copenhagen, sounded likely. He wrote thus:

The news of your fascinating idea have already spread to the Continent. Well, I get "Horse & Hound" every week and here I saw your interesting letter. How seriously I am interested, I shall explain later. I think that an introduction of myself will be useful in the first place.

I am the son of a Copenhagen textile manufacturer. I have spent 1½ years in Britain. That was from early '48–'49.

2. Plans and Preparations

I speak English, furthermore Swedish, German and some French.

As to horses and riding, I was nearly born on horseback. My father was always interested in riding, so I started riding at an early age, since then we got a farm where we now breed horses, thoroughbreds and hunters. Not on a commercial or big scale, but for our own use and fun. The whole family is riding and we have about five or six riding-horses and some draught-horses. I could explain much more, but that would tire you too much. I will finish saying that I had a very good time in England, from hunting in New Forest (10 hours) to hacking in Ireland and Rotten Row.

Coming home, I served my time in the Army in the Cavalry or Horse Guards for ten months, where I had a very good and educating time, what riding concerns. The last half-year I was in the remount depot where I had five horses to look after and ride. Now I am in business again.

You may say that I have wasted too much space on this information, and what interest should you have in a stranger's life and doings? Well, in spite of that I have done it, because you have now built up a picture of me, good or bad, and you know a bit of my background.

How much I would like to follow you can hardly be told in plain words—I know I could easily bear the riding, I would love the life on the road, I have tried it before, and my condition of health is superb. I know the Scandinavian languages, though not "Lappish." And I know rather much of the conditions, the scenery, the climate, the people.

*One thing I have thought of is, what do the various veteri-
nary authorities say? Will they allow the horses to cross the
borders without any time of quarantine? Are there roads that
way, or will we have to "pilot" us through the snow-covered
mountainous parts? I know from bitter experience how dangerous that can be in Norway on skis.*

Faithfully yours,

GORM SKIFTER

This letter was dated Copenhagen, January 18, 1951, and
emblazoned with the initials "G.S." on the notepaper. So as
G.S. I thought of him.

We corresponded again, questioning, advising, informing.
Wisely he wished to know what sort of fellow I was, whether
I knew what I was about, and whether I was determined to
carry it through. Meanwhile, I went ahead with preparations.

Equipment and clothing needed much consideration. At
best they could only be experimental, for I knew of no similar experience from which to profit. But I collected information of winter travel in northwestern Canada and Greenland;
and Scott's diary of his last expedition (surely the hardest
journey ever undertaken by man) gave useful hints about the
use of ponies in snow.

The experience of long-distance riders seemed to show that
a packhorse was needed and that meant a pack-saddle. These
proved as rare as a windjammer. But much probing in sad-
dlers' shops at last unearthed one, a relic of the 1914 war. It
was dusted and scraped, plied with saddle soap, and fitted

with new girths and breechings. It seemed that the best rid-
ing-saddle would be also cavalry pattern, as these were designed upon the experience of many years, for conditions
much nearer those to be expected than would suit a hunting-
or hacking-saddle, and they had the great advantage of being
adaptable to most normal shapes and sizes of horses' backs. I
got two of these saddles and leather pommel-wallets to go
with them. Bridles were also cavalry pattern, usefully combined with a halter. The only change I made was to have
snaffle bits for the Army reversible with its double reins: for
our purpose, the simpler the better.

For the first part of the journey, at least, clothes must be
suited primarily to the climate and secondarily to riding. Riding-boots and breeches were obviously insufficient. I had a
pair of Canadian flying-boots, the feet rubber, the legs leather,
and lined with thick sheep fleece that seemed ideal. Heavy
Air Force trousers seemed as good as anything and better
than breeches, for these would be too tight around the knee
with thick and long woollen underpants (also designed for
flying, and, I believe, the most cherished possession of any
traveller in extreme cold). I found a fur-lined jacket, very
Arctic-looking and warm, and proof against wind. To wear
beneath were layers of sweaters, a woollen shirt and vest,
and a couple of scarves. A heavy Cossack-like hat completed
a warm if somewhat cumbersome outfit. Changes of clothes
(I thought) must be taken, and, I admit with shame, pyjamas. A sleeping-bag, groundsheet, blanket, camera and films,
sheath knife, a small hatchet, and a copy of *The Compleat*

Angler were the other main items. Everything was kept down to what I thought at the time was the minimum, for every pound of weight would count. A packhorse must take dead weight, far harder on it than live weight, and a lightly laden packhorse could replace a tired ridden one if necessary. Thus, everything must be the lightest of its kind; even the smallest article was suspect. "On a long journey even a straw is heavy." I bought a midget and feminine razor with the trade name "My Lady's Boudoir," one quarter the weight of my safety. But upon trial it was obviously designed for more delicate operations than the felling of my bristles, which have unfortunately somewhat the coarseness of a flue-brush. I asked myself: "Is the convention of shaving really necessary or is it merely a fashion, done because others do it? Were men a hundred years ago any worse off for not shaving? Is shaving in ice-cold water a pleasure?" The answers were obvious; I gave away "My Lady's Boudoir." Then this letter came from G.S.

Yes, yes, and yes again. I am coming on the ride, subject to a permission from the military authorities from which I expect an answer very soon, but I trust this will go all right.

Your last letter and the information I have obtained later encouraged me very much. I have in the last week tried to get as much information about the northern parts as possible, and I have thinked over many problems. You say that we will have to cross the Muonio River before the ice breaks up. I have noted your opinion of shaving problems, my beard is

*not very fast growing, but it will save trouble and time not
to shave. The thing I am most worried about is the horses,
whether we will be able to get them in Norway, and how
they will stand the journey and the climate, especially at
night, but I hope for the best.*

*1. I think you know that you will have to obtain a visum
for crossing the Finnish border.*

2. How many horses will we need? (1 pack horse?)

*3. Are you able to go on skis? It might prove useful, and
we might want to do some skijöring, in order to spare the
horses for the weight.*

*4. What about some sort of weapon, shooting gun or so
(e.g. wolves are sometimes reported in these districts)?*

*5. About the route I would like to know whether you have
planned most of it, and I do not need to think more about
that or you would like me to make some plans?*

*I am definitely sure we will have many mutual interests,
and I am glad you know about mountaineering, but you
must have me excused, it is late at night now, so I go to
bed with the best hopes of hearing from you very soon.*

Such enthusiasm was welcome, coming from one who
knew the few possible hazards as well as the many pleasures.
One more letter and a cable made arrangements for our meeting in Norway. G.S. would come overland from Oslo; I
should sail from Newcastle to Bergen, and there we would
meet.

The ship came into Bergen early on a grey morning. There

was all the bustle and untidiness of ships that come in for early disembarkation, a hangover from the warm lights of the night before. Everyone who the day before had nothing in the world to do now rushed upon his private purpose.

G.S.'s train was due in about nine, so after breakfast I went on deck to watch for him and look for the first time at Bergen. It is a pleasant port, framed by tree-clad hills and coloured by its fishing; as in most ports, the dock area has the greater personality: old, interesting, and disreputable. Here is the fish market and the long row of Hanseatic buildings, wooden and medieval. Only on the hilltops was there any snow, and the air felt warmer than in England.

A taxi hurried upon the quay and drew up by the ship. Against its window leant a man wearing a Russian-style hat and an Arctic jacket. He got out, lean, fair, Nordic, and looked up searchingly at the ship. At once we felt we knew each other and smiled—apologetically at first in case we were mistaken, more broadly as we became convinced. We walked quickly towards each other along the gangway and shook hands.

3. Ship to the North

Nor shall Thule be the extremity of the world. SENECA

THAT night we took ship for Hammerfest and the North on the ruggedly named *Sigurd Jarl*. She was small and very clean. By morning snowless Bergen had given place to the piled snow of the Nordfjord Mountains, and soon we came into Alesund, a small fishing-town where tall wooden warehouses walled quays that suckled litters of wooden fishing-boats. Its smell was of salt and fish and tar. Soon there was Trondheim. Here summer clothes must be left for collection on our return by land: hopefully we went to the British Consulate. The Consul proved himself a friend and a character; thin, erect, with fine features emphasized by white hair and pointed beard, he was an English aristocrat out of the nineteenth century. Our escapade interested him. He knew Lapland well; years ago he had travelled many miles by reindeer sledge, going far across into Russia.

During the next four days we put in, with benevolent condescension, to some twenty fiord hamlets, many with only half a dozen houses gathered around their wooden jetties. You could have bundled each place, jetty and all, into the hold. When the ship came in, everyone—people, dogs, and cats—came down to these jetties to stand and stare and stamp. Our calling was as quick and easy and unconcerned as the visits of a postman, yet as incongruous as if the Flying Scotsman were stopping at a wayside halt to pick up a gipsy with a pig or a nursemaid with a perambulator. But winter had come down upon all approach by land, and we were their only means of intercourse. And always above these homely meetings was felt the presence of the mountains.

The second night out, as the *Sigurd Jarl* was setting course from Rörvik, we sensed this presence now hidden in the Northern night and felt the elation of the icy bluster from the *fjells*. As we leant upon the rail a glimmering came up behind the clouds lying upon the end of the sea and threw out the black of their rolling summits. It burst into flickering flames, a kaleidoscope of colours dancing before the black velvet backcloth of the northern sky, recalling the night of a bombed city with its ebbings and flowings of light. It was the Aurora Borealis, the "Northern Lights."

Next morning we sailed into the Arctic. The crossing of the Arctic Circle is far more satisfying than the crossing of the Equator. For one thing it is less worn, and once over the Equator you go, as it were, down a slope similar to the one you climbed. But you go over the Arctic Circle into an ever growing individuality of Nature, with the Pole as its climax.

As you go by sea the former is an unmarked, merely mathematical calculation; along this coast the latter is marked vividly by a stark and definite pylon upon a flat rock. You come towards it slowly—and suddenly you are level: then, satisfied, you say: "We have crossed the Circle—now we are in the Arctic." High above you there is a great jagged desolation of rock and snow and ice cracking the clouds that curl from its crevasses: the ice witches are brewing in their cauldrons. And everywhere above is the ice-green sky. Yes, you are in the Arctic.

So we crept punily northward past lofty Hestmannen, the "Horseman," which stands up from the sea like a cloaked and hooded rider, ever defying the snow hurled upon him by the winter's blizzards, an example and an omen.

Though Norway's fantastic winter coast often called us expectant upon deck, there was much to plan in our concentrated cabin, which thickened with tobacco smoke while the sediments of discussion piled high upon the ash-tray. How many miles a day could we expect from our horses? What kit need we buy and what could we dispense with? What was the plan should a blizzard hold us up on the Lapland plateau? What should we do if the unbridged rivers in northern Sweden were thawing and unsafe to cross? And, most important, should we take brandy or schnapps for warming in emergency? And, side-tracking, as G.S. had spent a year and a half in England, had I followed the New Forest Hunt? No, but I countered with the High Peak—and, said G.S., though the standard over open country was high in England, dressage was deplorable. With the latter I strongly and wrongly disagreed.

Five days out from Bergen the voyage came to its end. As the ship came carefully into Hammerfest harbour an icy wind reached down from the *fjells* to pull fur collars up around our ears and thrust our hands deep in our pockets. For here was the world's most northerly town and the snow lay heavy upon Lapland.

When the ship pulled in, a gangway was found to join it to the shore; men huddling privately in heavy furs walked on or off the ship; a sledge drew up, spilled a jumble of boxes, and slid quietly away. A similar load was let down by the ship's derrick and left in the mashed snow of the quay; there seemed no human interest in this traffic, as though it were a matter only between ship and shore.

Our kit sorted from the pile upon the quay, we heaped it possessively, sat on the tea chests, and lit our pipes. We discussed the little town that fanned out from the quay, guessing at the cosiness inside its heavy-timbered houses snuggling beneath their quilts of snow; we turned and argued as to which porthole had been our cabin's and remembered again the unlimited underdone roast beef, my national dish eaten without restraint for the first time since the war, on a Norwegian ship.

Suddenly G.S. interrupted: "Oh, did you see that sailor talking to me before we came on shore? I've talked with him a lot on the journey and as we were leaving he warned me to be careful as we're suspected of being spies and we shall probably be watched. Why they should pick on us I don't know, except that no one comes at this time of year unless they live here."

No doubt my eyes and mouth had opened in amazement as G.S. spoke, but fears quickly quietened by an easy conscience and the feel of a British passport in my pocket gave place to sudden shaking laughter. G.S. in his fur hat and sheepskin coat, myself with a quick-grown beard and high fleece-lined boots were too obviously the Russian spies of the Victorian thriller. And the two tea chests, splashed with strange Oriental characters, that we had watched with care on board because they contained saddles whose trees might be broken and so jeopardize our journey, asked for whispered speculation. So on the empty jetty, between the empty ship and the empty streets, two normally quiet men roared and rocked, while a pair of sea birds fled screeching from the *Sigurd's* rail, horrified by madness that laughed to find itself abandoned, with the boxes, on this Arctic quay.

A sudden shiver that was not from laughter told me that it was unwise to sit outside and the reason why there were no loafers here. Thankfully we saw an old man, leaning his weight against the towing-rope of a laden sledge, come trudging upon the quay. G.S. went to him and asked where we might find the boat for Bossekop; the old man stopped and straightened, and his arm went out towards a narrow funnel and a mast that peeped above the quay. We fetched a sledge that lay unwanted in the snow. I lifted a tea chest and, hampered by its awkward size, dropped it clumsily upon the sledge. "Mind the bombs," said G.S. and, the Bearded

Russian Spy vision returning, collapsed beneath his own load.

Our luggage aboard, we went to the saloon, which with its rows of wooden seats suggested the waiting-room of a bus station. Gradually a dozen passengers came on board for the six-hour journey up the fiord to Bossekop; some brought out food, others a pack of cards, others doubled up in sleep.

But to me all was interest. As we chugged out from Hammerfest I went out on deck and climbed the near-vertical ladder to the upper deck that was the roof of the saloon. And there, leaning upon the rail, was a gnome. He was scarcely four and a half feet high, with a grotesque hood, brightly embroidered tunic pulled in by a studded belt, legs wrapped tight in skins, and shoes turned up to a point. Walt Disney could have done no better.

Colourful peoples have always interested me. Now that most of them are throwing away their traditional clothing for a characterless international pattern, it is good to see colour and individuality, provided they have the backing of national history and artistry. Yet, however fantastically clothed, they had brought to mind nothing of the fabulous. But this Lapp did. Most of our fairy stories came from Scandinavia, and to the old Norsemen the Lapps were trolls and magic-makers; so they are the gnomes and dwarfs, the hob-goblins and elves (and later Santa Claus, when he took to reindeer). Suddenly to come upon a Lapp for the first time leaning on something so material as a ship's rail is a mingling of the real and the unreal which is fantasy at its best.

The Lapps are a unique and fortunate people, for they have almost escaped Hollywood, the musical show, and the woman novel-writer: how, God knows, for they are perhaps the most colourful people in the world. Should you wish to paint a Lapp as he is in his normal workaday clothes, you must use brightest blue for his hat and tunic, seam and embroider it lavishly with the vividest scarlets and sunniest yellows, encase his legs closely in reindeer pelt, put his feet in shoes of the same fur and turn up the toes fantastically to a point like Aladdin's, and bind them round the ankles vividly. You must wrap a wide gold- or silver-embossed leather belt around his middle and from it sling slant-wise a decorative leather-sheathed knife, and put upon his head a hat like one of the seven dwarfs'—or, if he be a Swedish Lapp, decorate it with a tassel like a prize chrysanthemum and almost as big as his head. For winter travel he will need a *peski,* a loose heavy coat of reindeer skin, brown, or white as the snow it protects him from. Finally, bring him from his reindeer-skin tepee and put him beside his sledge and antlered reindeer before a background of limitless snow—and you have him leaving on the 8:15; only he won't catch the five o'clock back because he's got to walk or sledge a few hundred miles across the uninhabited snows. But if he's not slowly stiffened by a five-day blizzard or trailed and torn and tattered by a wolf pack, he'll come back again sometime and put a tin on his fire for a brew of coffee.

He is of Asiatic origin, brother of either the Samoyeds of northern Siberia or of the Mongols. You see that often in his flat eyes and high cheekbones and his squat figure swathed in a reindeer-skin *peski*. Like most very small peoples, he is unbelievably tough and hardy—more so even than his neighbours the Finns and Norwegians and northern Russians, who are probably the hardiest of Europeans.

Yet they are a peaceable and kindly people. Should they happen to be at a village on a Sunday, they will gather their sledges around the little log church and in they will go with their dogs. No good Lapp leaves his dog outside: he is a friend and must not be left out in the cold, and why shouldn't he come in and talk to the good God, too? So in go the dogs and lie quietly at their masters' feet, and, good Christians all, they give thanks for their food and their fires and their deliverance from the winter's blizzards and the summer's swamps.

Many Lapps lead the nomadic life of their Mongol ancestors, following their reindeer herds to the *fjells* for the short summer, coming down to the lower lands for the winter. They follow the reindeer on skis, helped in their herding by fine dogs who look like crosses between sheepdogs and elkhounds. We saw later the value of their shoe toes, for there is no fumbling with a metal gadget on their skis but just a slipping of their feet into leather bands so that they seem to step onto the skis and are away all in one movement. It is said that the Lapps went on skis in the days of the Vikings long before any other race used them.

This practical reason for the curl in the Lapp's shoes is typical of all his clothing. His legs are covered tightly in skins so that no cold air can swirl up as with trousers; his loose tunic hinders no movement and by its embroideries tells another Lapp of his tribe; the *peski*, snow-proof and wind-proof, is made of the warmest material in the world— so warm that he may sleep in the snow in eighty degrees of frost and yet survive, for a reindeer, he will tell you, never dies of exposure. And with his slung knife he eats, stirs his pot, skins his reindeer, cuts his clothes, his tent-poles, and his thongs, and—on the very rare occasions when he quarrels in drink—fights. It is his cutlery, tool-bit, armoury.

This is largely the fascination of the Lapp. His picturesque life, customs, and clothes are normal and natural to him. The Red Indian puts on his feathers and war-paint only to enter- tain the gaping tourist; the Zulu bedecks himself to attract passengers to his rickshaw; the Arab drapes himself in clothes of many colours to increase his baksheesh. When they return home, they as often as not put on the creations of Brooklyn.

But not the Lapp. He does not masquerade for the tourist, for in the North he will not see one through all the winter, and if he is a nomad probably not even in the summer. Cer- tainly he has no use for international-style jacket and trou- sers. And often even the Norwegian or Swede who lives among the Lapps sensibly wears a *peski* and sometimes skin shoes and trousers when he travels in winter.

Snow clouds had snuffed out the stars and deepened the intense Arctic night as we came near to Bossekop. The spot- less white of the *fjells* could not be separated from the sky till you screwed up your eyes and stared long into the darkness—and even then you doubted. But the little ship came to the jetty and nudged it quietly. The pother under the stern ceased, the last circles of smooth ripples widened and stole out into the night.

4. Everywhere Snow

A journey of a thousand miles begins with one step. JAPANESE PROVERB

HERE in Bossekop the very start of the journey stressed its experimental nature by causing a change of plans that would have been unnecessary had we been able to profit from another's experience or been anything but tiros ourselves. Horses were few in northern Lapland and were not to be bought, but a captain of the Norwegian Army and Astri Tonberg, both of whom gave us great help in our preparations, cast round to find someone who might be persuaded to loan us horses and be our guide over the plateau. I believe our good friends thought us eccentric if not mildly mad, but, realizing our determination to proceed, helped us to the utmost by their experience of winter travel. They inspected our clothing and equipment, advising, adding, rejecting. They went with us to the store to buy emergency rations, snow-glare glasses, solid tinned fuel, storm matches and candles. Wisely they advised us to take a horse-drawn sledge rather than a packhorse, for over snow a horse can pull three times more weight on a sledge than it can carry on its back. In fact, a packhorse would have been useless, as we had to carry four days' fodder for the horses. They showed us how to dig in, should we be unlucky enough to be caught by a long-lasting blizzard, by digging a trench in the snow just deep enough to take us sitting up, just long enough to take us lying down, and roofed by snow blocks upon a timbering of skis. Then the entrance must be built up from inside, leaving only a hole large enough to pass an arm through, and a candle must be lit for warmth. When a vision of Bob Cratchit brought a smile, they assured us that in the small space the temperature would soon rise almost to freezing-point while a foot above our heads it might be sixty degrees lower; that more heat would melt the snow, and that one could survive for days in such conditions on emergency rations. It still did not sound very cosy—rather like sleeping in a refrigerator.

At this time of year no one goes to the plateau unless he must; our friends searched for three days before they found a guide and horses from Gargia, a short day's journey upon our route. He brought our riding-horses to Bossekop behind his sledge and took our equipment back with him, arranging to meet us there next day. He would come with us over the plateau to Karesuando on the Swedish border, where we should be able to buy horses.

We had talked much with the captain, a soldier of the old-fashioned school, alert, erect, and, even here in the North, smartly dressed in a quiet, soldierly manner. We asked him if they were not worried by the closeness of the common frontier with Russia; his smile in reply seemed to mean yes, but what could they do about it? "But," he said, "there is little danger of invasion in the winter. An army might establish itself in summer and build camps, but if it was caught in one of our winter blizzards—well, there would be little of it left. There is no village large enough to hold more than a few companies even if they turned out the inhabitants. Conditions were bad enough in the Finnish-Russian war in 1940; many men were frozen to death and neither side could make much headway, and that war was mostly fought hundreds of miles further south. Don't forget that here we are three hundred miles north of the Arctic Circle and the northern coast of Iceland, and further north than any part of the mainlands of Canada and Russia. It can become so cold that it may freeze a man's lungs—not here by the coast, but up there"— and he waved his hand towards the plateau.[1] "Geographically this is an extension of the tundra of northern Russia and Siberia—it shares with northern Russia in being the least-populated part of Europe; in fact, large parts of it are uninhabited, and here and there are areas unexplored and unmapped. You mustn't think of this as Europe but as the North."

At the time I thought he exaggerated, for we had seen many little villages along the coast and my Bartholomew's

[1] This cold and empty plateau, the Finnmarksvidda, with an area about the same as that of Wales, covers most of northern Lapland. Its scanty population is almost entirely Lappish, whereas southern Lapland (i.e., Finnish and Swedish Lapland, which extend southward to the Arctic Circle and beyond) is largely non-Lappish. No doubt this is due to the Arctic weather that prevails on the Vidda in the long winter, when it is swept by frequent blizzards.

map marked a good dozen places in the interior. But the next week showed my ignorance; the coast had been well served by shipping and was not truly Lapland, while some of the places marked on the map comprised only a dwelling and a stable, their *raison d'être* that they were convenient stages on a day's sledge journey. Galanito, for instance, boldly marked, was two Lapp dwellings with their store-sheds overlooked by a sentry-box-like privy on a little hill. Should the journey have left me with any doubts, they were dispelled by the reports of the two expeditions in 1951 and 1952 to Lyngen, an area southwest of Bossekop, where a large lake and glaciers were found that had never appeared on a map and *fjells* were climbed where no one had trod before, even their existence doubted by the people from the nearest habitations. Certainly it is difficult country for an invader with the paraphernalia of modern tanks and guns. Even further south to about 65° latitude Scandinavia is a country of mountains, forests, and bogs, with but one road from north to south in Norway and, apart from the coastal roads near the Gulf of Bothnia, one in Sweden also. Neither is better than many an English farm road, and loose-surfaced.

Our friends advised us as to the route as far as the Swedish border. We should go slightly east of south across the plateau to Kautokeino, the largest village of the plateau, thence due south over the tongue of Arctic Finland that juts towards the west, to Karesuando, on the northern border of Sweden. Here we must buy horses.

Lapland is beyond the reach of dusts blown from the deserts, and in winter the summer's dust is smothered by snow, so that the air is clear as bubbles in a beck. The low sun is piercingly brilliant and the stars hang big and close, undimmed by dust or damp. The night before our departure we went out to feel "the beauty of a Lapland night." The land lay pallid beneath stars that dulled the glow from two dwellings not yet abed, down by the sombre fiord. Before us the wall of the plateau cut short the display with a high horizon. A star shot across the immense sky. And over the plateau the night was glittering.

In the planning of an expedition there is sure to be anticipation, some pleasure stolen before the start. Two events will stand out as certain to be zestful: the start and the finish —the first swinging into the saddle, and the final vaulting to the ground (you would not merely mount and dismount on such gallant occasions). So we had thought. What did happen was that the beginning of the journey was to be a jog of half a mile to the local store to buy a tube of toothpaste forgotten in our shopping. As we saddled up, half a dozen people stood around, impassive but curious, where we had hoped for privacy to relish this moment. The saddle-girths proved too long and, there being nothing better, must be fastened high up under the flaps with wire. We fumbled with a pair of pliers in hands alternately clumsily gloved and miserably bare. This incompetence and lack of preparation seemed poor qualification for our journey. And when I mounted, the saddle twisted round, not far enough to drop me in the snow and raise an enlivening guffaw, but a mere foolish tilting that left me hopping on one leg while I wriggled the other from the stirrup. The saddle and its overloose girth were incorrectly dragged back, and my offside stirrup held while I mounted doubtfully, like a greenhorn at a riding-school. Then people said: "Good-bye" and "Good luck" in a way that meant they would see us again in a day or two, and went off to their homes and their fires, shutting their doors behind them on the cold. We started on the ride to the store.

Our equipment completed by the toothpaste, we mushed through the snow of the road, looking before us for the plateau's rim. But even this inspiration was denied us, for it was hidden in mist. We followed the prosaic tracks of the snow bus that goes now and then to Gargia.

The day was long and tiring, for we had not yet the philosophy of long stages that call for mental and physical readjustment for their appreciation. At noon we missed the comfort of a warm lunch and the easy-chair that sometimes follows it. And the distance we covered was so ludicrously trivial in relation to the whole journey, and, apart from the cold, a ride might have been more eventful in Rotten Row. But at Gargia *fjellstue* [2] we were cheered by the sight of the plateau's edge, now near and clear of mist, and a hot meal of reindeer meat, and went to bed feeling that even if we were fools we were at least to be happy fools, which was all that mattered.

Early next morning the guide Per came in to wake us apologetically and say that the sledge and the horses would

[2] Mountain hut.

be ready in an hour. Obediently we dressed and ate. Per had done this journey before on reindeer sledge, and just as we relied on him to follow the trail, so we thought it wise to accept his time-table, for his slow, quiet confidence was assuring. He was taking a companion with him as company on his return, for he did not care to cross the plateau alone.

When we went out, the sledge was already laden with food and clothing for the horses and ourselves and with the tea chest containing the pack-saddle, kit-bags, a bucket, shovel, skis, and *peskis*. The sledge-horse, like the riding-horses, was a Döler, the north Norwegian breed, powerfully but not heavily built, with a strong arched neck and broad chest and quarters. He was loose and chased around like a dog, scattering snow from his hoofs, tossing and shaking his head and charging us from time to time for the fun of seeing us jump aside. The lack of shagginess of these horses was surprising, as they lived further north than perhaps any other breed of horse. Yet they seemed to carry less coat than many an English pony in winter, and when we saw them finish a day's hard travel of thirty-five miles in the snow with heads still high and as aggressively as they had started, we wondered again at their hardiness. They seemed made of iron. Though it was of small matter, they were poorly schooled by accepted riding-horse standards and took little notice of conventional aids. They were trained to halt to a rolling of the tongue that sounded like *"Brrr"*; at first this seemed vaguely amusing, till it occurred to me that in this temperature it had an aptness that was perhaps not quite so funny.

Beyond Gargia the solitudes begin. Almost at once the trail wound up the rim of the plateau. As it went higher the conifers of the coast became stunted and shrivelled, giving way to the small and hardy Arctic birches with their branches scoured by the blizzards standing out sharp against the snow. The trail, laid down in layers by the falling snow and pressed hard by sledge-runners and the hoofs of reindeer, was fair going for the horses. The winter way over the plateau follows, not the summer route, but the ruts of the first Lapp sledges to cross after the first snowfall, and often its route is blazed along frozen lakes so that many miles of it goes straight as a rule and level as a table. For part of its distance it is marked by birch branches or posts that stand up gauntly at intervals of perhaps a quarter of a mile to guide the Lapps in a blizzard. Once the trail is left, there is little hope, for in a blizzard a man will wander in circles as if he were lost in a mountain mist. Even a compass is of little use where there may be but a single dwelling in an area of five hundred square miles and visibility is that of a London fog. Finding the needle in the haystack would be simpler.

Early in the afternoon we came out at last upon the plateau. Soon Per, who rode with his companion on the sledge, reined in his black Döler and suggested that we eat. When he fed the horses, G.S. and I were surprised to see him give each one a half-bucket of mixed oats and snow, and feared colic; but this is normal diet for these hardy horses. We had much to learn.

: 38 :

We stood by the sledge, grateful for the *peskis* now that we were still. Though a low, clear sun shone upon us, the effects of altitude made themselves felt and we hunched deeply in the furs, stamping our feet. The air from the comparatively warm currents that creep upon the coasts and keep open most of the fiords had not come with us to the plateau. Per said: "This plateau is known as the 'Vidda,' which means 'wide'" (we thought it appropriate). He nodded towards the west—"Over there is nothing until you get over the mountains to the sea. Over here to the east is nothing except Karasjok and half a dozen Lapp dwellings till you come to the Russian border. Apart from the Lapps with their reindeer, nothing lives up here now but the wolves, and they sometimes die of hunger and are eaten by the others. If there is anything left, the crows eat it in the summer when the snow has melted and given place to swamps. It is no good to anyone." And he looked at us, wondering why we should come here at all. Yesterday we had wondered that ourselves, but now the cold air, almost effervescent in its vitality, had filled our lungs. This was the kind of journeying we had expected, and today we had not missed our comfortable lunch.

Dusk was falling as we left the surface of a long lake and came to a dwelling hibernating in a hollow with its stable, the first habitation since leaving Gargia. It was solitary and apparently without reason for existence; but there was a reason—shelter for travellers by reindeer sledge. Indeed, in the almost one hundred miles from Bossekop to Kautokeino there are but two habitations apart from Gargia near the start of the journey.

A Lapp came into the sleeping-room with an armful of birch logs and dropped them by an ornamental black stove built in tiers so that it had something of the shape of a wedding-cake. With his knife he peeled off the bark, heaped some of it upon the bars, and stacked the logs conically around it. When lit, it flared and spluttered while he fed the growing flames with more bark till the fire roared, for birch-bark is full of resin. This was a lesson in firemanship that proved useful to us.

Next day we came to the utter emptiness. Empty of life, empty of sound, empty even of the stunted bushes, an infinite flat whiteness cut in two by the trail. Over this desolation the puny caravan crawled insignificantly as a maggot.

Yet that sledge took on a ridiculous importance. It carried everything we owned, everything a man could possibly need: food, clothing, tobacco, a copy of *The Compleat Angler*. It was our hub, our metropolis.

When sometimes G.S. or I rode on ahead or dropped behind, our sledge reminded us of the Kon-Tiki raft as seen by its crew from their dinghy. Yet it was not in the same way amusing; there was no painted sail, no shelter of branches; everything was very plain, very utilitarian, with no touch of colour upon us but the shred of embroidery on Per's *peski*. In these solitary sorties you felt the silence. I realized I had never known silence before. The calmest sea had always lapped quietly upon its shore or been disturbed by an unquiet ship; among mountains there had always been a movement of the air or a distant rumour of a stream; the desert had had its cricket or the shifting of its sands; but here was an absence of sound as though it were frozen and blanketed by the snow. But for its whiteness and its coldness this snow desert might have been a flat sand desert; there were the same wind-made ripples, some in lines like miniature rollers curling upon a beach, others rhythmic and delicate in twists and twirls, accentuated in their clinging shadows. Though the brilliant sun hung low in the sky, these were the only shadows but the caravan's, shapeless and transitory. For here is nothing else to cast a shadow.

5. Blizzard and Blindness

Blow, blow, ye winds, with heavier gust!
And freeze, thou bitter-biting frost!
Descend, ye chilly, smothering snows!

BURNS

G.S. and I were often callous about the other's lesser difficulties. As trouble for one might be a photographic scoop for
the other, the fortunate one considered it unsporting should
his less fortunate subject free himself before the click of the
camera.

Today I was riding ahead of the caravan in one of my es-
capes to solitude, when the trail divided. The right-hand
branch seemed the more used, so, without waiting for Per
to catch up, I followed it. Soon there came a hail from the
sledge and arms waved towards the other trail; I rode back
and, as the sledge came level, thoughtlessly cut across the
few yards between us. At once my mare sank under me almost to her belly and plunged and reared in fright. I jumped
off, sinking halfway to my knees, and clambered back with

: 42 :

her to the hardened snow, where she stood and rolled her eyes in disapproval. But G.S. was delighted. He had been about to photograph my return along the trail when I gave him this better material. This incident showed the need for a guide, for Per told us that the right-hand trail led only to a Lapp camp twenty miles away; it was No Through Road and would have added a couple of days to the journey to Kautokeino and so left the horses seriously short of food. Also it showed that only the trails made a winter crossing of the Vidda on horseback possible; we carried horse snow-shoes—circles of cane some ten inches across on a metal framework, similar to the check of a ski stick—but these were for emergency only and would hardly enable a ridden horse to go easily in snow.

When domestic man halts in the open for any purpose, it is usually by some feature of Nature. If there is a single rock in a desert, a tree on a mountain, or a stream in a valley, then it is ten to one he goes to it before unpacking his lunch. Perhaps his living in houses and towns makes him feel uneasily small and exposed in the midst of vastness. So yesterday we had fed the horses and ourselves by a cross standing from a heap of stones. Today there was no landmark; only time and hunger decided our eating, and we rested only long enough for the horses to eat their hay and oats.

Soon after we started on our way again, a dark speck grew upon the horizon and at last moved slowly towards us. Then it broke into segments and we saw that it was a reindeer caravan, long and plodding. There were perhaps a dozen sledges in single file, each reindeer tied to the back of the sledge in front. Upon the first a Lapp sat motionless: on the caravan's flanks two more went in the long, flexible stride of men used to soft going. Both parties halted while Per and his companion spoke with the leader. Here G.S. had to rely upon Per's interpretation, just as I had to rely upon G.S. for interpretation of Swedish and Norwegian. Our Lappish was limited to the greeting *"Bouris, bouris,"* which is accompanied by an arm upon the other's shoulders. This is magic with a Lapp, warming his face, for it is the age-old welcome of the Vidda, of men sharing solitude and possible peril.

But G.S. and I found interest enough in the reindeer. They surprised us by their small size. My ideas, at least, of reindeer had been formed when I was a small boy by the exaggerations of Christmas cards and placards of Santa Claus outside department stores. On the average, they are little higher than a Shetland pony and no heavier. Frail in appearance, they are quick and enduring and pull a sledge thirty miles in a day on an armful of sage-coloured moss and then sleep contentedly in the frozen snow and sixty degrees of frost. This moss is their only food; sometimes it is baled and fed as hay, but when they are in herds they dig for it unerringly in the snow. They have no need for snowshoes, for their wide hoofs are well suited to going in snow. The reindeer is everything to the Lapp: food, clothing, and means of exchange; to ask him how many he owns is a serious blunder, for it is asking how much money he has. The thought came to me that, just as the snow and sand deserts have their similarities, so have their inhabitants: there is this dependence on their herds, and their nomadism or semi-nomadism with its seasonal migrations to better grazing, its frequent tents, its tribal system, its hardiness and fatalism, its common sense mixed with superstition, and a love of colour as relief from the usual monotone of their land.

As we parted from the Lapps they drew their caravan from the track to let us pass. My mare seemed unused to reindeer and certainly had no liking for them, for as I led her past she frisked and reared, twisting around me while I held tightly to her bit-ring. And when I mounted she stood rigid with curiosity till I dug in heels and urged her forward.

I do not like discolouring the world by looking through tinted glass, so I often carried my glasses in my pocket. To-day the sun's glare had sharpened and the snow became a blinding ubiquity of light so that I screwed up my eyes against it till they began to ache and a sudden pain struck across my head. I let the reins fall and pulled the glasses from my pocket; but the headache stayed with me for the day as a warning.

We saw snow-blindness later. Per's fine Lapp dog (spelt very much with two p's) had been tireless on the journey, chasing before us on the track and out in great bounds upon the snow at either side and leaping back at the horses with gleeful barks. He must have gone a good fifty miles a day. He was a grand dog and would, I believe, have torn the throat from any man who laid hands on his master. Like all living things but the horses in this hard land, a mass of fur covered a hard and wiry body. Sometimes we looked and there was no Cherkis but a frenzy of legs in the deep snow whence came growls of satisfaction. Then came a vigorous showering of snow from a now vertical Cherkis and a boisterous barking and chasing after the caravan. So when he began trailing quietly behind the horses we thought he was tired at last. But when G.S. turned in his saddle to talk to him, he shouted to Per: "Look at old Cherkis; his eyes don't look too good." Half closed, they blinked and watered; he looked unhappy and in pain. We stopped. And with a dog's intuition he knew the reason and came quietly with his head bent to his forelegs and bushy tail trailing upon the snow and pushed an eloquent head between his master's calves. Per lifted him upon the sledge with the gentleness that hardy men often have for their dogs, took off his *peski* to lay him on, and covered his eyes with a sack. Poor Cherkis: he gallantly wagged his great bushy tail in thanks, but even his stout heart could not suppress a low whimpering as pain piled up behind his eyes.

Our destination that evening was a Lapp dwelling standing squat and solid in the snow, its heavy unpainted logs interlocked at the corners in the Finnmark fashion. The walls inside were of the same natural logs but decorated here and there by brightly painted cupboards and Lapp clothing hanging from nails. Reindeer steaks, and ceaseless mugs of coffee brewed in a kettle on the black stove, were lavished upon a rugged table. The Lapp tried hard, but without success, to understand why we should travel here on horseback rather

I. *Arctic port—"litters of little fishing-boats"*

II. *"Pylon upon a flat rock"*

III. *The author and his horse*

IV. *G.S. sets out on a journey*

v. *"A cross standing upon a heap of stones"*

vi, *"The puny caravan crawled"*

VII. *"My mare seemed unused to reindeer"*

VIII. *A caravan arrives at Galanito*

IX. *Halt near Kautokeino*

X. *"Stating simply in four languages"*

XI. *"Waiting for the ice to melt"*

XII. *"A lonely charcoal-burner"*

XIII. *Old stables near Arvidsjaur*

XIV. *"A bright orange sunset lit up the pines"*

xv. *A Lapp village*

xvi. *Marshes*

than reindeer sledge. We were regarded as a man would be who rode a yak round Piccadilly Circus. No one, he told Per, had ever ridden across the Vidda in winter, and he showed its folly by telling us of three men who rode into the Vidda: two were exhausted by a blizzard and died; the third tied himself to his horse, which brought him unconscious back to Bossekop. But he offered a practical hint by recalling how in one of the historical sagas a blizzard-bound traveller had saved himself by slitting open his horse from throat to chest and crawling feet first into the warm carcass, from time to time cutting pieces from it to sustain him. This seemed about the most repulsive tale I had ever heard; but if a man were faced with this or death by freezing, which would he choose? I do not know and hope I never shall.

Next morning the intense cold of the past two days had gone; instead there was almost a mildness in the air and Per's thermometer read only fourteen degrees of frost, so that G.S. and I loosened the scarves from our necks and stuffed gloves into our pockets, joined in our rejoicing by a now recovered Cherkis. But Per looked about the horizon without content. Some people are never satisfied, we thought, and went on in the beneficence of the sun.

But we had been barely an hour upon the trail when there came a slow greying of the sky along the horizon to the east, creeping upon the sun. While the grey ate away the blue, a movement in the air began to break up the stillness and blow the dry snow about the horses' feet, lightly lifting their manes and rippling their tails. The sun was dimmed and at last put out, and a coldness struck down at us, wrapping scarves once more around our necks. Frozen flakes which had drifted low like sand blown along the seashore began to rise with the wind and swirl about the horses' heads and then ours and above us we knew not how far. Now the temperature, which had gone down steadily since the coming of the cloud, suddenly dropped as if the bottom had fallen from it. The silver line on the thermometer withdrew into its bulb like a snail to its shell as the wind wailed up to a gale. It was reading 63° of frost and still it fell. We dismounted and went beside the horses to ease the numbness of our bodies, bending our heads and almost shutting our eyes against the flogging of the blizzard. We half covered our faces with our scarves till our breath froze upon them and stuck them to the skin. We pulled them painfully from us. Then the snow crystals blew into my beard and set solid upon my jowl. Certainly there was little comfort today upon the Vidda.

We were a silent company; once or twice we tried to speak cheerfully, but the cold went down our throats and strangled speech, so that the only communication was by insistent search from near-closed eyes for dark movement, an outline of a man and a horse, or a sledge and a horse's straining shoulders. We went together in a cell walled by swirling snow; today we did not wish to go alone, for that would not be freedom, but confinement. At intervals a gaunt pole or a doubled-up and quivering branch loomed wailing into our cell, passed by us, and faded out behind.

There was no thought today of lunch, only a resolve to

come out of this blizzard; no other thought, only numbed feeling: the feeling of your face set hard as in cement and now anæsthetized by cold against the stinging of the storm; the palsy of your arms, one set stiff as a cripple's, the other crooked tensely round your reins. Only your legs felt the pulse of blood; powered by the will, they thrust forward heavily.

We went slowly and laboriously, for, as Polar explorers have testified, the battering of a blizzard exhausts both mind and body in a strange and insidious way. If a man comes to the limit of his endurance (which is probably more mental than physical), he will give way to the irresistible desire for sleep and lie down in the snow. But it is a sleep from which he will not awake.

In the afternoon we came to what we feared to find— places where there was no longer a trail, the ruts filled in and smoothed out by drifted snow. At first it was for a few feet, then yards, and I wondered whether we should have to dig in and how we could shelter the horses. By standing the sledge on its side and buttressing it with the tea chests perhaps, but this would be poor shelter. Several times the one in the lead paused to bend down and look for the trail; once or twice we could not find it and went on carefully in hopeful search.

But at last towards evening the blizzard seemed to weaken. At first we dared not hope lest it be a pause to gather greater force, but now we went upright where before we had leant upon the storm, and the white wall had gone back from us;

so when a pale light filtered down from the sun we turned one to the other in relief that cracked the frozen skin around our eyes. Soon the sun came down brightly and thawed out the stiffness from our bodies; the snow blew about aimlessly for a while before settling lightly upon the ground. The blizzard was over.

At evening the trail came out upon a long and frozen lake. The sun was already falling from us, washing the shelving eastern shores in gold. As we rode, separately now because speech was discord, lake and low hills changed subtly to rose and to red, and deep cold-blue shadows reached out longer across the lake. An early moon as big as a dinner plate stood against the sky upon the ledge of the horizon. The stillness had crept back behind the storm, and there was no sound in the world but a soft rhythmic crunch of snow beneath the hoofs.

As we rounded the bend of the shore, a caravan of reindeer sledges trailed towards us, led silently by Lapps. The white and the blue, the red and the yellow of them were the snow and the shadows and the radiant hills; the cold, crisp tinkle of the reindeer bell was ice. Man was playing in harmony with Nature, point and counterpoint. As we passed, no one spoke; only were there grave liftings of hands, for this was not the time for hearty greetings. Now I thought that I understood why the Lapps are nomads and that I knew the reason for their peaceful minds.

Gradually the lake narrowed to a river that sank slowly between its banks and all was ever-deepening blue and once again the cold cut sharply through our furs. At last, as we came round the bending bank, it uncovered lights one by one and revealed Kautokeino, lonely settler in the snow.

Kautokeino competes with Karasjok, which lies some eighty miles away, for the title of metropolis of the interior. They are the centres of trade, communications, administration, and social life, and give their names to (or take them from) two of the largest Lappish tribes. In Kautokeino are two or three dozen wooden dwellings, a Lapp church, and a store, scattered over an area of perhaps a square mile, for even the settled Lapp comes from nomadic ancestors and likes a little space around him. Straight, compliant rows are nothing to him, for he leaves herding to his reindeer. The street knows its duty to the houses and goes among them usefully and by night curves beneath its lights brightly as a string of tinsel. In the eight winter months it is a wide, well-hardened reindeer track, for even the most ambitious motor car could not come here, so that the only mechanical vehicle that Kautokeino had seen in winter was a light caterpillar-track similar to those used by Greenland expeditions.

On the night of our arrival in Kautokeino we looked down from our window into the village. The street ran sparkling beneath light that dimmed the windows of bordering dwellings to a mellow amber. Now and then a door remote from the street opened to silhouette for a moment a bulbous figure black upon yellow, and to let out for it a carpet of white along the snow. And then down a slope of the track there slid a sleigh along the soundless snow, drawn by a tall and dashing reindeer flaunting his antlers high. A Lapp upon the sleigh, gay in scarlet and yellow and blue, crouched forward from his furs to flick the reindeer with his whip. And as they went by, a sleigh-bell tinkled. It seemed unreal, like a stage scene from a pantomime beneath its brilliant lights; it was fairyland and Santa Claus. I cannot say that he drives his reindeer over roof-tops or drops down chimneys, for these we never saw, but no one can tell me there is no Santa Claus. That is a lie told by parents to their children.

6. Arctic Finland

Donde una puerta se cierra, otra se abre.
(When one door is shut, another opens.)
CERVANTES

THERE was ill news in Kautokeino: a serious horse disease had broken out in Finland and a ban had been put on horses' crossing the frontiers. At first we planned to put snowshoes on them and turn westward off the trail a few miles before the border to join the trail that runs along the Muonioelv and so come to Karesuando as though from the Swedish northwest. But, regrettably low as was our respect for laws and frontiers, reflection showed that we might spread the disease, and this we were not prepared to risk. It seemed that the best plan was to go as far as we could towards the border so that we should be on the spot, and then we could work out a plan to cross over. Certainly we were too far away at Kautokeino. We must go to Galanito, the last habitation before the Finnish border, whence Per, his companion, and his caravan would return to Bossekop. We should be as near the frontier as possible, and here we hoped St. Hubert would provide. I must explain about St. Hubert. G.S. had a personal interest in him as the patron saint of huntsmen and considered that we should put ourselves under his auspices. At first I objected on the ground that he was not the saint who dealt with this kind of thing, that we were not at the moment bona-fide huntsmen, and that we ought to be under the protection of the saint of horsemen in general. But G.S. pointed out that we were qualified by our following of well-established hunts, that he knew of no saint who looks after horsemen in general, and that I was being pedantic. So I gave in, with secret doubt as to its correctness.

To Galanito was an uneventful journey that rose gradually from the Kautokeino valley towards the plateau once more and ended when we dropped down suddenly to Galanito in a hollow.

Here we stayed with a Lapp named Tornensis, who owned one of Galanito's three dwellings—which, with their outhouses, are more self-supporting than most countries, for the birch trees, the plots of summer land, and the reindeer provide everything. The rest of the world could be hydrogen-bombed and devastated, but Galanito could (and probably would) go on as before.

The log-cabin-like interior was very plain, with a black stove that warmed and cooked, a rough and bulky table, cupboards, and short, wide wooden beds like vast dog-beds. For ornament there was an old alarm clock with one hand and no glass, and a photograph of a film star, the treasured memento of a journey into Karesuando. Beside each house was a meat-rack set high upon stilts beyond the rapacity of wolves and foxes and reached by a rickety ladder. There reindeer meat was dried in the summer sun and preserved by the winter cold, hanging in black slivers like dried bark, repulsive in appearance but retaining all the rich flavour of uncooked meat and similar to South African biltong.

A Lapp has little to do in the snow-bound winter unless he is travelling by sledge or tending his reindeer herds, so that Tornensis and his wife and two children seemed to do nothing but cook and eat and smoke and look at their strange guests. There was an old, hardy man about Galanito; what he did or which house he lived in we never knew. He wore his *peski* with the hide outside and fastened round with a broad and studded belt, so that, with his face wrinkled and leathery as his *peski,* he looked like the "wild Lapp" of the Elizabethans. Usually when we saw him he was sitting in Tornensis's house by the black stove, grasping a great hunk of dried raw reindeer meat on the bone and about the size of a leg of mutton, slicing it with his knife, and champing upon it with uninhibited delight. When at last he had finished for a while, he thrust his knife down in the sheath that hung from his broad belt, licked his chops joyfully, rubbed the back of his hand across a wide and satisfied mouth, and rolled his eyes at us in glee. He was a lean pattern of Falstaff and we liked him immensely.

The day after our arrival the good St. Hubert provided for us. A reindeer caravan was about to leave for Finland and would return in two days' time. Its Lapp leader, bleary, droop-eyed with alcohol, and a notable winter traveller, promised to have a guide and horses from Finland waiting for us on the frontier on the third day. He would be back in Galanito on the second day and the next morning he would provide fresh reindeer and take us to the frontier.

G.S. turned our forced wait to advantage by writing, for he had been commissioned by a Danish paper to send reports from time to time on our journey.

On the second day he was sitting industriously at a rough wooden table; I was lying glumly upon my back on the scanty comfort of the wooden bed and staring up at the too familiar markings of the roofing-logs, and then down to a brightly coloured wooden figure tied to the foot of the bed. This, we had been told, was a charm against the Uldas— goblins or trolls who live beneath the ground, herding their fine reindeer: to hear the bells of these reindeer is an ill omen. Also, it seemed, the Uldas have an irritating habit of taking human babies from their beds and substituting their own. (For my own part, I put more faith in a somewhat leathery appearance than in a charm, for the Uldas are fastidious in choosing only the most cherubic of children.)

Having nothing better to do, I began to consider for the first time the odds on the journey. True, we had come most of the way over the plateau, but not all, and beyond that were four hundred miles of the Swedish forests and the Kiolen range to cross before we came to Norway. What if we were not allowed to take horses over the Swedish-Norwegian border; suppose there was an import duty we could not afford? And, thinking of horses, we hadn't even bought them yet. Would it be easier to buy them in northern Sweden than it had been in northern Lapland, and if not, what then? And if we lost one through an accident, or one was taken by wolves or a bear? (As is usually the case with fears, none of these happened, though, strangely, one or two unexpected events were to come as near to disaster.)

Then I wondered how long we should have to wait here. The Lapp had said he would come back in two days, but we already knew that time has no meaning to a nomad Lapp. Perhaps it would be two days; perhaps two weeks. He would not mean to let us down, but hurry is unknown to him. After all, we had food and shelter and tobacco—what more could a man want? Suppose, too, he was caught in a blizzard? Or by a pack of wolves? I felt like a prisoner of war waiting for the war to end he knew not when. In fact we were almost prisoners, for we could scarcely hope to take our saddles and kit to Karesuando without reindeer, skis, or a tent.

A knock sounded on the door and a tall man came in, stamping snow from his Lapp shoes upon the threshold. He was clothed in a reindeer-skin coat, shorter than a Lapp's and held in by a wide leather belt, Lapp trousers, and a hat of wolf pelt. A rifle was slung across his back.

He spoke to me in Swedish, of which I yet know only a few words. G.S., seeing my difficulty, took over and they talked for a while. When he went, G.S. did his best to answer my curiosity, but he was little wiser than I. "He's a strange fellow. He's trapping and he said he'd heard from the Lapps that we were here; but Tornensis obviously did not know him. He was quite interested in our ride, so perhaps he's a reporter in disguise"—and he went back to his writing with a grin while I lay back on the bed again, suggesting feebly that he might be an Ulda.

On the evening of the third day there was a sudden jingle of reindeer bells, and from the window we saw our guide-to-be and his team breast a ridge and then come sweeping down upon the house. We went out into the snow to meet him. Tomorrow we should be on the way again.

At dawn we set off bravely at a smart trot. A fine buck pulled our guide's sledge, to which was tied a hind reindeer following with a transport sledge that suggested a cross between a child's play-pen and a tumbrel of the French Revolution, and that was now laden with our saddles and equipment. I followed, and G.S. brought up the rear. It was a trim little caravan.

My sledge was very comfortable and I lay back luxuriously among warm reindeer skins with a careless air, for what was a bit of reindeer-driving to a horseman? The single thong that did duty as reins, one end tied round the animal's neck, would scarcely have seemed sufficient for a horse, but a reindeer was a puny thing. I turned and grinned happily at G.S.

We had gone perhaps half a mile when a dog sprang out it seemed from nowhere and chased up to us, barking boisterously. I hailed him, for I like dogs. But not so the reindeer.

Suddenly the sledge lurched forward, throwing up my legs and banging my head on the back. At once we were in a gallop, a swaying, one-runner-at-a-time gallop, the reindeer's hind legs showering me with snow while I hauled on the thong, cursing and commanding in a tongue foreign to the reindeer. Though our course was erratic, the dog could not keep up the pace and stopped to watch, his tail wagging gleefully. At last the reindeer stopped dead and looked back malevolently while I waited foolishly for the caravan to catch up. It is doubtful whether G.S. or the dog laughed the louder. From that moment I have regarded reindeer with deep respect: weight for weight, they will beat a horse any day, and all on a bit of moss. They must be as active as any living thing but a flea.

Soon after we left Galanito the oasis of stunted bushes gave place again to the snow plateau, flat and white and empty. Again space, and so time, was unmarked. The lack of partitions to divide them into sections makes travelling unconscionably long: you look around for some object—a hill, a tree, even a bush or a stone, which you may reach and leave behind and so feel progress. But there is nothing. So when we saw a pinhead of darkness before us, we took off sun-glasses till the snow-glare puckered our eyes, and the Lapp saw our curiosity and told us that this was a heap of stones which marked the frontier. As far as the extreme edge of the horizon there was no other indication that here you came to another country, for there was nothing in Nature to mark it.

The Lapp halted his reindeer by the cairn, lit up his roughly carved pipe, and sat impassively, his small, far-seeing eyes set upon the forward horizon. Soon G.S. and I began to fidget in civilized impatience and asked him when he thought the horses would be here, but he said: "They will come" and lit his pipe again. The Lapps knew long before the scientists that space and time are infinite: long journeying across empty wastes had told them that.

But at last he took his pipe from his mouth and pointed towards the line that separated sky and snow. We accepted his silent word that these were the horses. Soon we were piling our kit upon yet another sledge, and we followed it and its Finnish driver out upon the trail. Once or twice we looked back and saw the silent Lapp and his caravan shrinking to a speck that at length seemed to be sucked down into the snow. Our Finnish ponies strode out sturdily, cheering us that we were mounted again, so that time went more quickly. Soon the sun sank, fiery and immense upon the rim of a cold, white world. Its red heat emphasized the ice-cold blueness that soon spread across the snow, now held in the stressing of silence that comes with dusk, so that it was as though we looked upon a primeval ice age before the start of life.

Night had fallen when we came to a rough-logged dwelling and its stable huddled protectively together, their dark outline the only break in infinite whiteness. And everywhere vivacious stars scattered a pale light over Arctic Finland.

The next day was mildly exciting, for it should see the

completion of the journey over the plateau and bring us into Sweden. This prospect and a sprightly sun made a talkative morning, so that an alien mark of darkness upon the snow was at first of no interest to us. But when we came to it and saw that it was a pile of reindeer skins it took on sudden importance. We dismounted and pulled off the top pelts, half in curiosity and half in fear for what we might see there. It was relief to find that they covered only other pelts, but this did not answer our question. That they had belonged to a Lapp was certain, for only he takes skins across the Vidda. But where was he? No one would willingly leave thirty or forty valuable reindeer pelts as an old hat thrown aside, and such a load could hardly have fallen from a sledge unnoticed. There seemed only one explanation: the blizzard. Perhaps a Lapp caught in the storm had jettisoned his load and lost his way upon the snow. But no such traveller had passed through Galanito, nor, as we found later, through Karesuando.

Towards the end of the day we came into rolling country varied by occasional pines and firs. Our guide was leading, hunched upon his sledge; G.S. went next, and I followed. Several times G.S. had looked round, traversing the horizon as though to imprint the scene upon his mind now that we were leaving it. Again he slowly turned his eyes, past me— and just past, they stopped. Doubt seemed to flare up for an instant: then there was sudden conviction. He pointed and shouted: "*Varg!*"—and as I turned curiously—"Wolf!" It was loping a quarter of a mile back along the trail, resembling an underfed Alsatian dog. We yelled to the Finn, who started from his thoughts, looked round, and pulled in his horse. The wolf also stopped and slowly crouched. The Finn looked around him as though searching for others of which this might be the leader or a scout. The wolf rose on his forelegs, threw up his head, and howled—a drawn-out howl like that of a dog in pain—then slunk through the snow and disappeared over a rise. From time to time as we rode along the trail we heard distant howls; our guide told us that there was probably a small pack following on our flank in the hope of a horse separating from the party. But they kept out of sight in the now undulating country, for wolves will rarely attack men except in extremity of hunger. Most wild animals know that man, physically the most defenceless of creatures, has strange and deadly weapons that it is wise to avoid.

In the late afternoon we dipped down from the plateau and saw below us the broad belt of the Muonioelv and the little wooden villages of Finnish and Swedish Karesuando, the latter pierced by the wooden spire of the most northerly church in Sweden. A wide track cleared of snow joined them across the frozen river, and when we came down to the northern bank we said farewell to our guide and piled our kit by the track, for we could not take these Finnish horses across the border. Two boys offered themselves and their sledge to carry our kit and satisfy their curiosity; saddles on our arms, we walked over the ice to the border post on the far bank. Here they opened the crate that contained the pack-saddle; they looked in our kit-bags and examined the small axe and *The Compleat Angler*; they looked at us. Obviously they must decide whether we were bad or merely mad. After debate it seemed they decided the latter: they swung back the red-and-white-striped barrier and let us into Sweden.

7. South to Sweden

Widespread they stand, the Northland's dusky forests,
Ancient, mysterious, brooding, savage dreams.
Within them dwells the forest's mighty God,
And wood-sprites in the gloom weave magic secrets.
HEADING TO THE SCORE OF SIBELIUS'S
SYMPHONIC POEM, TAPIOLA

AT once we made inquiries for horses. Yes, there were a number in the neighbourhood used for pulling sledges and hauling timber—but horses to ride? They smiled, amused. So we went around the outlying *bruks*, without success until we met the government veterinary from Vittangi. He had heard of horses that might suit us and went with us to a *bruk* some ten miles from Karesuando. A yellow-dun Finnish mare was brought from her stable into the deep snow. I liked the look of her and went over to see if she was sound; with more energy than sense, I jumped on her back to find if she had been ridden. She had not. She had never known the indignity of a man jumping on her back and she would not tolerate it now. She had stood eating oats for a long time in her stable, and the crisp air intoxicated her. As I picked myself from a snowdrift I thought that not only was this a most comfortable place for a fall if one must fall, but that this horse more nearly resembled an eel than any I had known. She, on her part, stood trembling at this sudden assault without warning or even the formality of a bridle. But I liked this horse: I liked her alert head with its wide nostrils and restless ears, her strong barrel carried on fine, wide-set legs, her heart near her hoofs. She was the right size for the job, a little over fourteen hands—not too small to carry weight, not too large to have stamina. And it is a good, strong colour, this yellow dun with a black ray and points. It seemed unlikely that we should find one broken to the saddle, so in any case a few days must be spent in schooling. At last our luck had changed: next day G.S. found a horse to suit him, a dark-bay gelding about the same size as my mare, immensely strong and short-backed, quite without fear of human beings, but with a persistent curiosity in their doings. The gelding was called Musti, diminutive of *musta,* Finnish for "black"; the mare Pilkis, from *pilkku,* Finnish for "spot." (She had a white star on her forehead hidden beneath her black mane.) Musti was the younger, rising seven, and Pilkis was nine—both good ages for our purpose, for they were young enough for resilience and old enough for sense and stamina.

Unfortunate though it seemed at the time, we could not now afford to buy a packhorse, for horses had proved expensive; so we had to resign ourselves to doing without. The training of the horses was a problem; normally we should have expected it to take six weeks, but as we had to be on our way, five or six days was the limit. We gave the horses an hour's lunging and long-reining three times a day and spent much time with them in the stable, feeding them by hand and stroking them and talking to them so that they became used to us. Nothing was left undone that would cause them to connect our presence with pleasantness, such as teaching them to follow us round for titbits in our pockets. On the third and fourth days we saddled them and took their hay outside the stable, and while they ate, we leant upon the saddles, gradually increasing the weight until we lifted our feet from the ground, so that they became used to it while content at their hay. At last we leant right across their saddles on our bellies; then we held pommel and cantle and levered ourselves up by straightening our arms; and then gently turned round so that we sat sideways in the saddle. Now very gently we stroked their shoulders and then their flanks with our feet and moved our position slightly about in the saddle. From this position it was easy to slide our feet over their necks and so into a riding-position in the saddle. Then one persuaded the other's horse, with its rider in the saddle, to follow for oats so that they learnt to walk with their riders and to regard it as pleasant.

One afternoon we had walked back over the frozen Muonio to Finnish Karesuando on the far bank. Its dozen or so houses, a store, and a primitive café were grouped about the mashed surface of the snow-cleared street. More from curiosity than from thirst we went into the little café: it was empty and very plain, with a temporary, utilitarian air about it like a canteen on a war-time gun site. When we ordered a couple of bottles of beer they were brought to us without glasses, and our asking for them was met with a kindly tolerance towards these foreign fads. The beer was first puzzling, then indifferent, then nasty; simultaneously we offered half-empty bottles across the table in the hope that what was nauseous to one might be bearable to the other. It was not. We likened it to vinegar and water and went out sadly into the street.

It is, of course, impossible to know anything of a country by spending an hour or two in one of its villages, but we did notice a guarded aloofness about this place; people did not seem to group together in the street or in the store as is the way in Scandinavia, but went about singly and quietly as though not certain who was the patriot and who the Communist. It is, of course, not many years since this country (whose real name is Suomi, not Finland as it is known in many foreign countries) was part of Russia: since then parts of it have twice been invaded by Russia and once by Germany, so this doubt is easily understood. Indeed, over all the extreme north of Scandinavia there seemed a quiet alertness, due perhaps in part to its tangled frontiers and an emptiness that was suspect because it was hard to watch. The sensitiveness of these frontiers was well expressed by a report we heard in Karesuando: recently a man travelling on skis had misjudged the boundary and was found ten yards inside Russian territory. He was fined the equivalent of five pounds —expensive travel at ten shillings a yard. Only the Lapps seemed indifferent, with the nomad's disregard of man-made frontiers, for they are a thousand years behind us and perhaps a hundred years ahead.

As we went back to the Swedish bank a cloud hung like a morning mist above a bend of the *elv*. Slowly it moved towards us and from its van a handful of reindeer darted momentarily, to be swallowed again by the forward-rolling cloud, the breath from thousands of panting, dilated nostrils. At last the reindeer won the battle for leadership and came out on a broad front; hoofs rose and fell like myriad pistons, and antlers tossed above the broad brown bank of reindeer. Now and then a straining group lunged forward, only to be caught up and merged once more in the mass. At last the leaders swarmed past us, followed by thousand upon thousand going it might be fifty wide or a hundred, like an army in review, now trotting, now cantering, for perhaps a quarter of an hour, officered upon their flanks by Lapps crouched urgently upon skis. As they went up the *elv* the cloud seemed once more to overtake them, leaving only a broad and churned-up swath to mark their passing. It was one of the great seasonal migrations towards the *fjells*.

The day before we left was a busy one. The pack-saddle that had been cherished as indispensable was left with the customs officer to be sent on later to our port of embarkation in southern Norway. A drastic culling of kit was necessary, for apart from the many clothes we wore, everything was to be carried on the saddles, either in the saddle-wallets or strapped to the dees upon the cantles. All was turned out upon the floor: on one side were gathered the necessities, on the other the desirables and the luxuries. All were suspect; even an article of a few ounces was not immune: keep one and you keep a dozen, and soon that means pounds instead of ounces and all to be carried every step of a thousand miles. Finally there was left the following:

Blankets to go under the saddles and on the horses' backs during the march, or, if the horses were stabled and we slept in a barn, on our backs at night. Unhygienic perhaps, but practical.

Strapped to the saddle-dees:
  Groundsheets and sleeping-bags, neatly rolled ("Sleeping-bags" is perhaps a courtesy title; G.S.'s could be crammed into a good-sized pocket; mine was a sewn-up blanket.)
In the obligingly expansive saddle-wallets:
  Cameras and films
  Small towel
  2 pairs of socks each (holeless except for the heels and, later, the toes)
  Handkerchiefs
  1 tie (mine)
  One or two horse medicines, to be shared if necessary by the riders

Journey from the Arctic

Toothbrushes
1 tube toothpaste (shared)
1 piece soap (also shared)
1 brandy flask, empty but kept with unquenchable faith
Biro pens and scraps of paper gleaned from various sources
Maps (Bartholomew's and, when we could get them, large-
scale military)

In pockets:
Passports, money, diaries, and large reserves of morale with
pipes to smoke it in

Finally we each took with us one concession to habit: in my case pyjamas, in G.S.'s a minute down pillow about a foot square that was each night patted and placed ritually on hay, boards, grass, or rock. The pyjamas were not long to be with us, but the pillow was kept almost to the end of the journey, despite my jeers and sneers, which always came up loudest from a neck stiff with lying upon a saddle or the hard earth.

Spare vests and pants were jettisoned, or what G.S. termed "thrown." On the face of it this was unhygienic, highly uncivilized, and quite dirty, but in fact we were able to wash the pair we kept from time to time and leave them scorching overnight above a stove in a *bruk,* or later, in the summer, to wash them alternately and drape them domestically from the saddle in the sun. Although we carried rather less than the average week-end hiker, yet strangely we had all we needed. We were indeed amazed to find how much could be done without and how much is due to habit rather than need: certainly the simplifying of life that comes from few possessions is considerable compensation for poverty.

The Muonioelv is final. From its northern bank the emptiness of Finland and northern Lapland reaches out to the Arctic Sea; southward from the other bank there is four hundred miles of forest. It is a natural as well as a political frontier, the limit beyond which the pines and firs do not grow except as crochety individuals in sheltered hollows.

As we left Karesuando we turned for a last look at the plateau, a wild, weird terrain that had fascinated us and was never entirely understood. Then we rode into the forest: forest, because there is only one, split by frozen rivers and stabbed by lakes and rare human dwellings that pack it like moth-holes in the pile of a carpet. You go over the lakes and rivers, and again the curtain of firs and pines closes round you. Further north you feel infinitely small in a vast vacuum; here you feel larger because this dull-green circular curtain goes ever with you; in the extreme North you see nothing but snow because there is nothing else to see, here you see nothing but trees and the snow about their feet. This does not mean that either is unpleasant or even lonely; loneliness of a philosophical kind you may feel, but not the desperate loneliness of being alone in a city—say in going by London tube during the devil-take-the-hindmost rush hours when you yourself are going nowhere in particular. Though we found travel through this at first claustrophobic forest objectively monotonous, yet subjectively we were never bored. We had many of the things that breed content, such as the health of physical exertion with its resulting tiredness at the end of the day, and the achieving of a purpose, for every step was a brick in our house and we enjoyed the building of it.

The solitude of these forests is almost as complete as the Vidda's, for in Sweden, as in Norway and Finland, human life is grouped in the south, where are the busy capitals and the industry. Along the road from the north are three towns in as many hundred miles, yet even these can be termed towns only by comparison with the solitude that surrounds them, and their populations are less than that of many an English village. Even by the road you can go twenty miles without sign of habitation; by the tracks which we followed whenever possible you may go forty. But even a track will always bring you somewhere, sometime.

For parts of the journey we had military maps; when these failed we fell back on the Bartholomew's, where a good day's journey covered half an inch, or relied upon information from the last *bruk*.

The first day we rode along the slopes of the Kuormak-kafjell, which stands up alone from the forest. It was a day of dreadful wind, chasing down behind us from the plateau and blowing up a stinging drift that cracked our lips just healed from the blizzard. We thought with longing of the *peskis* that Per had thoughtfully brought for us upon the sledge, and hunched sullenly into our fleece jackets, cursing their inadequacy.

The second night was experimental. Foolishly we slept on, rather than in, the hay in a barn, with groundsheets beneath us insulating us from the warmth of the hay. We shivered through a sleepless night with time for reflection upon the techniques of barn sleeping. In future we made trenches in the hay and heaped it back on top of us and left the cold groundsheets anywhere but next to us.

When your watch tells you it's past ten o'clock and the horses tell you it's time to stop, then, unless you believe that there is food and shelter around the corner, it is best to look for such shelter as Nature may provide and at least rest if you cannot eat. So when on the third night out from Karesuando our military map told us there was neither, we cast round for shelter among the trees. Five closely clustered firs offered hospitality; we cut branches from their less friendly neighbours and laid them crosswise to keep us from the snow and on top laid one of the groundsheets to complete a mattress. The other groundsheet was slung between two of the friendly firs upon the straps from the saddle-dees and its other end was tucked beneath the mattress to form a lean-to with its back to the wind. Perhaps it was not the cosiest bed we had ever slept in, but remarkably good in the circumstances.

We slept one at a time, for there was not enough clothing to keep two warm and it might be unwise to leave the camp without guard. G.S. slept the first watch, undressing by taking off his boots both for comfort and as a concession to custom, and wriggled and groused his way into the sleeping-bags till he found a place where his hip-bone did not lie hard upon a branch.

I gathered dead branches and cut them with my knife, piling them by the bivouac. The twigs were too damp to light from a match, so I cast around for paper. A much-read letter, the fly-leaf from *The Compleat Angler*, and four pieces brought with civilized inhibition from Karesuando were carefully crumpled and stuffed beneath the kindling. The flame rose and fell and then crackled up in cheerful blaze, brightening the encampment by its ruddy flickering upon the trees and the snow and inclining the horses' heads towards it in appreciation. It sizzled and spluttered, eating down inside a grey circle of mush. But perhaps its greatest comfort was in the knowledge that wolves fear fire: horses tethered at night were a tempting bait. We had heard at the *bruk* the day before that a pack was hunting in the forest and had killed many reindeer. But for its weight, we should probably have carried a gun of some kind that would have given us sport and food if nothing else; as it was, our armaments consisted of a sheath knife (G.S.'s) and a Swedish dagger (mine) with a sharp edge and fine blade, used in place of a more orthodox knife. As neither of us was called Tarzan and we were not travelling before the cameras in a studio, these were perhaps inadequate; in any case, we had more faith in a few burning branches and a flood of abuse if administered at first sight. Yet imagination kept me fully awake as I sat on a fallen tree and smoked, or paced up and down to keep warm, while the moon set shadows slinking among the trees and an occasional crackle from the fire snapped the tense hush of soundless snow. But in the morning the sun came out cheerfully along avenues between the trees.

Today the stowing of our kit was not easy and suddenly my pyjamas became suspect as parasites, for it seemed that barns and the open air were to be our usual bedrooms. The top I would keep as a spare shirt (though it was later torn up as bandages for Pilkis's legs to support her tendons after a long march), but the legs seemed worthless vanity. In foolish whimsy I tied them head-high to a fir sapling, where they blew out bravely in a collaborating breeze; for all I know they still fly there, grotesquely striped, above a squashed-down bed of branches and a grey-white circle of ashes.

Next day we came to the Törnelv, the last of the un-bridged wide rivers, and rode over its frozen surface and up the far bank into Vittangi.

Here we found that our friend the vet had returned the day before. He introduced us to a largely Danish family who entertained us royally with friendliness and food and drink, while in their honour G.S. and I wore our Best. This con-sisted of a washing of the once-white laces on G.S.'s heavy ski-boots so that they stood out smartly, and my wearing, in place of the usual scarf, an enormity of a yellow tie decorated with horses' heads and a recent tobacco burn the size of a shilling.

8. The Forests Close In

. . . Unless your journey be a plaguy long one, and if so, never ride your horse more than five-and-thirty miles a day, always, however, seeing him well fed, and taking more care of him than yourself; which is but right and reasonable, seeing as how the horse is the better animal of the two.

GEORGE BORROW

IN the morning you woke quickly. There was no disinterested dawning as in a familiar panorama at home, long ago memorized and since unnoticed. The new and unusual roused your eyes: never again would you see this bed-place; tomorrow's would be another and different. Depending on the type of quarters—bedroom, barn, or bivouac—you noted a colourful cupboard, hand-carved and painted, a pair of skis leaning lankily, a garishly painted plough, a sad rat-eaten *peski,* a wolf pelt, a grotesque tree or a quaint snowdrift that raised a simile.

But soon, writhing from its restriction, you sloughed your sleeping-bag and woke the other with push or shout, ungraciously received. The first-booted went to the horses. They stood alert and expectant, heads raised to neigh at the meaning of your arrival. They were led to water and, wet-whiskered like seals, led you urgently back to an expected mass of hay and its nucleus of corn. When unhappily there was none you patted them foolishly, feeling mean and shamed by their surprise. Useless apologies were followed by a cowardly retreat from their disillusioned eyes. You always wished you could explain to them.

But usually there was food. Should it be a mile from us, we smelt it out, and by hook or by crook it was the horses'. Then we found their earthy company more soothing to an empty morning stomach than our own or each other's. This is no reflection on G.S.'s good company; I have always found it so. Give me a horse before breakfast every time.

You returned to find the other tousled and aimlessly just out of bed. (You couldn't see yourself, as you had no mirror.) He was fiddling with wallet straps or a groundsheet. You started resignedly on your own and somehow got in the same mess yourself, though you saw ample excuse, for everything went against you in the morning.

Should snow, a beck, or a well be handy, there was a hasty washing of face and hands, in my case followed by a determined drinking of cold water (a habit begun in the tropics but halved in the Arctic). G.S. was scornful of this display of English hardiness, but I remained resolute in sin. It swills down the still-hot clinkers of yesterday's nicotine and is the first step towards brightening today.

Both G.S. and I unwillingly had to admit that we had lost all military efficiency. We had served in horsed cavalry regiments—successfully, we recalled, relating feats of tactics and horsemanship with merely moderate exaggeration. But, for the life of us, we could not get away in a time worthy of an idiot. Meagre kit had to be squeezed into even more meagre wallet, and that meant a system, a putting of things in places suited to their nature and shape. Finally there was the holiday-maker's departing dirge: "Now what have we left behind?" Then we would state that in the Army we used to do all this and more and be smartly mounted and raring to go in a quarter of an hour (or whatever it was). Now an hour went by from our rising to our going.

One night G.S. had rumbled up from the hay that sprang high upon his chest: "Y'know, it's time we got away quicker in the mornings; we waste no end of time. Let's organize things and make a system tonight." I agreed heartily. Everything would be put in its place, in its right order; no time would be wasted. Now our Army training would show what it could do. Next morning G.S. started us precisely by his watch. We worked feverishly, grimly, silently. We saddled triumphantly. G.S. looked at his watch, making a quick calculation. In perplexed monotone he announced our time: "Fifty-three minutes." Next morning we went back to our unhurried, disorganized couple of hours, content to recall those Army days.

There was nothing that could be called conversation until we were on the way; only low, frustrated cursings, sometimes

of oneself, sometimes of the other; monosyllables from bent
and tousled heads:

"Where the devil's that bucket?"

"Don't know; never seen it."

"Have you got the soap?"

Answer as before.

"Dammit, that's my pipe."

No answer; a grunt.

At last: "Well, are you ready?"

"Yes, been waiting for you."

Resigned silence. You knew that you were always the one
who waited.

When you exercise heartily all day, it is bad to stay awake
until one or two in the morning talking with puzzled hosts or
arguing plans for the morrow, as was our habit. The instincts
of the horses told them that: weighted by their evening meal
and grunting their content, they let their legs slowly and
stiffly collapse beneath them like the leisurely closing of a
pocket-knife and sprawled out into sleep, their outstretched
legs and heads and the accentuated rotundity of their barrels
giving them a strangely camel-like appearance. Rarely does
a horse relax into the cosy curling of a cat or a dog. But as
they sleep early, they wake early—bright and clamouring
for food. So, early to bed, they woke more healthy than we,
wiser and no less wealthy. The only excuse for our addle-
witted morning moods is their human prevalence. Probably
a sense of humour and philosophy (which are largely the
same) are the best purgatives, but these virtues often sleep in

for a while after the body is afoot. But always we knew that once upon the road our imbecilities would be shaken loose by the jog of the horses and blown away by the cheerful wind and we should laugh at ourselves for having given them paltry room, for, like germs, they do not thrive in the open air. So a morning that awoke in the forests to the smell and rustle of pines, the matins of birds, and the greetings of the horses was too healthy to be a breeding-ground for wrangling. St. Hubert was compensating us for an empty belly.

Should we have slept in a farm-house (and often also if we bedded down in the hay), an invitation would come to us for breakfast. This caused a further hour's delay, as our hosts had had time to think of further questions, and manners and gratitude forbade a hasty leaving upon the emptying of the plates. Once we did apologetically refuse a breakfast to save a valuable hour, but only once. A familiar growing hunger throughout the day brought home our folly, and each of us, silently and aloud, swore a great oath. We easily stood by it.

Always the household turned out to see us go upon our way, and often there was regret at the early parting of new but good friends. We shook sincere hands before fetching our horses and again as we left, bending down gallantly from the saddles. G.S. no doubt phrased his thanks eloquently; I made up for quality by quantity, repeating vigorously *"Takk, takk so mycha; takk, takk."* As we left, we turned often in our saddles to wave, at last reaching high in a long-arced sweep. I fear we must have looked very Hollywood, though not so tidy.

Along the way the sameness of the forest threw us increasingly on mental or oral entertainment, or sometimes both. In this vigorous air you could not jog sleepily along in the cud-chewing relaxation of an English summer lane, deliciously doped by earthy smells and the crooning of bluebottles. (I must hasten to state that I am not libelling bluebottles: I like 'em and would do them no wrong. They are the soothing accompaniment of warm English summer days, the minstrels of sultry, shimmering waters, of ferns and foxgloves in scented woods, of village-green cricket matches. Their crooning is that of the concise *Oxford Dictionary's* "To hum or sing in a low undertone," not its "cf. Dutch *kreunen* groan," as in fashionable usage.) So, alternately, we rode together or tired of talk, one dropped behind the other for thought upon the journey and everything else under the sun still we drew together again for its liberation. We rarely agreed comfortably upon plans for the journey: when G.S. thought we should go to a place thirty kilometres away I saw every reason why the one twenty kilometres away was inevitable; and when I saw clearly that a broken track was our only way, G.S. knew instinctively that it was impossible. So, plans for the journey disagreed upon, we drifted into talk of everything else: shoes and ships, cabbages and kings. Only sealing-wax escaped. Here we found that our ideas and values, our likes and dislikes were largely similar; we could be bores without boring; we charmed each other by our knowledge and good taste. We were, of course, well placed for oratory, for the horse has a presence and aristocratic tradition sadly lacking in a soap-box. Wellington would have given little dignity to spacious canvases had he stood before Waterloo, one among many: Alexander, Charlemagne, Saladin, and Genghis Khan, all the makers of history were behind us. And we were fortunate in our audience, for from three hundred miles of spell-bound trees came not one dissent. Occasionally, when the air became too strong for speech, we sang to them lustily, as we would not have dared before humanity. But later, towards Norway, we were to ride in longer silences, for mountains are less easily intimidated than trees; the speaker becomes the listener and goes in awe.

One of our greatest problems was to keep the horses fit on the irregular feeding that was their lot. A horse will lose condition more quickly than a man on meagre food and with more serious results. He must travel every yard by his own energy, where his rider may relax in his saddle and make smaller demands upon his flesh. Because the horse has a small stomach, he cannot carry a reserve of food; thus the horsemaster's rule for feeding is "little and often."

The clear midday sun was now melting the snow in patches; bright blades of grass sprang up, small and scanty as yet but full of the vitality of spring, the horse's natural food designed to counter the winter's ravages upon his flesh and well-being, to stuff him full of proteins and vitamins and thus round his quarters and clear his eye. So upon the march we looked out for these oases in the snow, dismounting for the horses to pull at them eagerly. When possible we kept to a march routine: each hour or so we dismounted and slackened the girths to rest the horses for five minutes, while trotting or the occasional canter was limited to the same length of time, for walking does not run the flesh off a horse as does a faster pace. Now and then we walked to ease their backs and stretch our legs and warm us, looping reins upon the pommels and training them to follow at heel like dogs. Rare opportunity for giving them a midday rest and a feed at *bruk* or lumber camp was never missed, for we seldom knew when the next feed would come. Thus, progress was never fast, but there seemed no virtue in making records. Careless horsemanship would have weakened the horses so that they might have failed on at least one future occasion when times were hard; and there was the pleasure far greater than any high m.p.h. of finishing one-and-a-half thousand miles with horses as well filled out and in far harder condition than at the start five months before.

Most of the time the going was extremely hard for the horses; first snow, then bogs, then the *fjells* with their often rugged tracks. It is doubtful whether more than a dozen miles of the journey was across fields. Half of it was snow or rock.

Anyone can ride fifty miles in a day once he has learnt to relax in the saddle and the skin of his seat has become as calloused as his hand, and some think it fine to "ride my horse to a standstill." They might try doing the fifty miles on their own feet and see how tough they feel then. But this sort would find good reason for stopping after the first ten. The only saddle for them is that of a bicycle.

The time came when we had to press the horses beyond reasonable endurance, but this was to bring them and us to food and shelter. Then the horses were rested for a couple of days and carefully fed. They travelled anything from ten to thirty-five miles in the day, not a high average over easy country and on regular corn, but there was neither. Most European horses would have gone to skin and bone in a month, and we were indeed fortunate in our hardy horses from a northern stock that is a survival of the fittest and a near relation of the basic Mongolian pony that thrives often on dried bushes and snow.

The second day out from Vittangi brought more Spy Trouble. Whether the suspicions of Hammerfest had been handed to the Swedish authorities we did not know and probably never shall; only do we know that the police and military took more interest in our passage than it seemed to require.

So upon a stretch of road cleared by snow-plough, an Army car pushed by us and pulled up. We rode to it, interested in this rare encounter by the wayside. Two officers came from the car and stood authoritatively across the road: we reined in.

"Your passports, please."

Mine was studied; the officer suddenly looked up and there was a rapid exchange of questions and answers.

"Are you English?"

"Yes."

"What part of England?"

"Cheshire."

"Where's that?"

"South of Manchester."

"What do they do at Old Trafford?"

"Play cricket mostly."

He handed back my passport; they bade us good-day and drove off in the car.

Five minutes' thought and discussion as we rode upon the way told us it was no accident that we were stopped: few Swedes are so knowledgeable of Manchester, or of cricket.

Our destination was a hamlet down by a frozen lake. We knocked upon the door of the largest of the four dwellings. Again we knocked, and a face snatched at the window to be swallowed at once by the darkness within. This was an unfriendly and suspicious day. We regarded each other, weather-worn and outlandish; and, understanding, led the horses down a foot-pocked path towards a primitive shack. Here the door opened to our first knock and we were welcomed by a man of obvious Lappish features, yet dressed poorly in a ragged overcoat and trousers and a cloth cap. He went before us to a rickety stable half buried in snow, horses and men sinking to their knees, and eagerly shovelled the snow from the door. As we led in the horses he disappeared, coming back almost at once beneath a heap of hay. The horses settled, he hurried us back to his shack and a cauldron of meal. From time to time he exploded with his arms into speech, belching strong tobacco smoke from a heavily carved, unpolished pipe; in his pauses he looked without interest before him. He was the only Lapp we met who had no composure; the only one dressed in European clothes; the only one away from his people. Probably the latter two explained the first; he was trying a less elemental life and finding it disturbing; the nomadic ways of life were too strong in him for change. Whether the hope of money had attracted him or whether he was an outcast from his people he did not say and we could not ask; but either he would rot of discord or of drink, or go back to his tribe. I hope it was the latter, for he was kind to us.

We slept in a great box of a bed like the one at Galanito, beneath a pile of reindeer skins, and in the morning rode away upon the thirty miles to Gällivare, little twin town to Kiruna which lives in the wilderness eating away a mountain of solid iron ore.

Here an outlying *bruk* found stabling for the horses and ourselves. For experiment we slept in straw instead of hay, and to all potential barnstormers I say if you want warmth, use hay. Certainly straw is cleaner and you are not plagued by elusive hay-seeds between the shoulders, but it is better to itch than to freeze. A good scratch may be satisfying, but shivering never.

9. Forests and Food

Hath not old custom made this life more sweet
Than that of painted pomp? Are not these woods
More free from peril than the envious court?
Here feel we but the penalty of Adam,
The seasons' difference; as, the icy fang
And churlish chiding of the winter's wind;
Which, when it bites and blows upon my body,
Even till I shrink with cold, I smile, and say,
"This is no flattery: these are counsellors
That feelingly persuade me what I am."
Sweet are the uses of adversity;
Which, like the toad, ugly and venomous,
Wears yet a precious jewel in his head;
And this our life, exempt from public haunt,
Finds tongues in trees, books in the running brooks,
Sermons in stones, and good in everything.

SHAKESPEARE

SHOULD you travel southward from Gällivare, you will
know of its isolation. We rode twenty miles without seeing
even a *bruk,* a hut, or a square yard of tilled land; everywhere
was unused forest standing silent with its feet in the snow.

Then we came suddenly to a log hut that brought hope of food and shelter; but it was barred against the winter, callous and unsociable. So we went on with the traveller's immortal hope that ever expects shelter around the corner.

About ten o'clock there came out to us across a frozen bog a track of stirred-up mud and snow. At its unseen roots a solitary roof varied the forest with a dab of red among the green. We reined in and looked. . . . We must try. The horses squelched and sucked till they came out into a clearing where stood a farm-house and a stable. We dismounted and knocked. There seemed no life. Again we knocked, made more determined by rising doubt, and again, till at last the door creaked carefully open and a man in a *peski* over flannel pyjamas craned out his head suspiciously. G.S. spoke with him at much length before convincing him of our harmlessness.

The horses stabled, we went back to the house. The living-room was bare and smelt as if its air had been let in months ago before the cold came, and now, run-down and tired of use, was brooding at the windows till they opened and gave it freedom.

His wife had come down and now padded round in flapping slippers to put humble food on the table. She was blowzy and dressed in a thick once-white nightdress which seemed to cover day clothes rather than replace them, suggesting blasphemous Bolshevik cartoons of saints. We slept in an attic, the only upstairs room apart from our hosts'. But they had come from their beds to give us all they could, freely and without thought for reward: a king in his castle could have given no more.

Two days later we approached the Storaluleälv, the river that empties the Stora Lulevatten, one of the great lakes drained from the Kiolen Mountains that wall off Norway from Sweden. When it is waked by spring's warmth it stirs beneath its ice, splitting it and hurling it from the Harsprønget *foss*, tossing the piled-up floes to the rocks below, shattering and ricocheting them into blocks and splinters at last to be eaten away insidiously in its warmer reaches towards the sea.

As at Gällivare, so at Harsprønget, Nature had brought men into the backwoods by her wealth; a dam was being thrust across the river where it rushes to the falls, to gather together and pile up its dissipated power. Authority, feeling the nearness of the Iron Curtain and its habit of lifting its hem furtively to let out prying agents, had slung its own curtain around Harsprønget. So we were doubtful as we rode along the western bank towards the prohibited area.

Gradually and with no realized beginning there stole into our senses a low rumbling as from an upheaval deep in the earth. "Now we must be near the falls," we said, and rode on searchingly. But the forest still contained us. Soon a new and loose-gravelled road ran across our course; we turned out upon it and stopped to read there an uncompromising sign, stridently yellow: "Entrance Forbidden." Soon came others: "Smoking Forbidden" (we hid pipes obediently in our pockets); "Prohibited Area"; and then: "It is forbidden to enter this area under severe penalty." This was threatening, and it huddled us in debate. Against proceeding: there was no cleverness in trespassing, and we did not wish to cause official suspicion that might jeopardize the journey. For proceeding: we were set on seeing the falls to best advantage, and a belief that bluff can take one serenely in the knight's move over officialdom's rule-bound pawns; finally and decisively, to go back would waste the greater part of a day's journeying.

Came more notices, larger and even more urgent; then suddenly a couple of workers. We behaved as though we were old mates of theirs and nodded in a friendly manner towards their astonishment and said it was a lovely day and that the falls had never looked finer and the job seemed to be going on very nicely now. We passed by amiably and almost at once the trees cleared and there was the dam reaching out across the wide river, and upon its incomplete end a gaunt crane; beyond, a flimsy bridge jumped the gap. Very soon we climbed the steep slope of the dam and came at once into a group of workers. The advantage of preparedness was with us, and before they could question us we launched into badinage and friendly platitudes, walking our horses quickly but without hurry, counting each step a gain until we were out of hearing and went on at a faster pace painted with indifference. Curiosity tugged at our heads to look and see if we were followed, but we set our necks rigid and looked only to the turbulence pouring from the gap.

The crane dominated the dam like a lighthouse upon a headland. Here we were at a disadvantage; we could not see into the crane's cabin, which perched like a nest in a winter's tree while we were as naked upon the dam as a liner on a summer sea. The advantage of surprise was no longer ours; questioners would have recovered from indecision and be seething with suspicion. Sometimes we turned up eyes beneath our brows, but still there was no movement. It seemed now probable that the crane was idle, and when at last we rode beneath the tangled girders we knew our luck still held. So far it had been as easy as riding across a field and now there was only one Rubicon—the bridge. Success had elated us and we regarded the bridge with confidence. Certainly it was a crude affair: wooden floor and rails and barely six feet wide, but held up by beams as thick as a man's body. We dismounted.

Musti was led to it: suddenly he jibbed and started back, terror bulging his eyes. G.S. quieted him and tried again. Again and again he refused, snorting like a bassoon and trembling back on his hocks. Sweat broke out along his neck and was lathered up to a white slime by the rubbing of the reins. We dared not say it, but each thought, and knew the other thought, that we had fallen at the post, that we must go back—and that probably meant trouble this time.

Neither of us considered trying to whip them across, for in panic they would as likely as not charge through the flimsy rail and plunge down in sickening somersaults and be swept away as helpless as beetles in a mountain stream. Musti had always been so phlegmatic and had walked so imperturbably along the dam that we felt this sudden disappointment the more keenly. And there was our goal, only fifty yards in front. To hide disappointment rather than from any hope I shouted: "I'll try Pilkis, she might go." G.S. nodded dispassionately, knowing the uselessness.

With the bridle loose in my left hand but my right ready to grab her bit-ring with all my strength, I led her onto the bridge, saying quietly: "Come on, old girl"—and droned to her, into her ear: "Yes—it's all right, old lass—there's nothing to it—easy as walking into a stable—yes, it is, old girl"—and all sorts of stupidity besides, for words did not matter if the tone was soothing. But though I affected a leisurely indifference to soothe a horse's receptive mind, inside I was as shaken as the bridge beneath us. And she went as quietly as going into a stable.

Then after immeasurable time we stepped onto the bank and turned round to see Musti pawing and fidgeting, lifting his head and blowing out his nostrils in inaudible neighs. Concentration setting his face, G.S. took up the reins; the horse's fear of isolation was strong in Musti, and after a flickering hesitation on the brink he ventured the bridge, stepping high as if it were hot to his feet. When almost over, he suddenly took fright and leapt into a canter, crashing against the rail, which whipped sickeningly, leaping onto the bank, dragging G.S. by the reins; then he stood still and looked meditatively at Pilkis with mixed shame and respect.

This was our first intimation of a queer reversal in our

horses' characters: Musti, it seemed, hated bridges, while the high-strung Pilkis was indifferent. So in future Pilkis led over bridges, encouraging Musti to follow. We sat restfully for a while by the bank, taking in the splendour of the falls, before going upon our way.

An unruly track took us through the forest to Ligga, marked boldly on our map. We had become used to its filling-in of empty spaces, so it was no surprise to find that Ligga consisted of three *bruks* with dwellings and stables all bundled into a clearing of less than a quarter of a square mile.

A peasant woman of half-Lappish appearance welcomed us to her dwelling. It was poor and dirty but hospitable. Upon a grimy wood-fired stove she boiled a cauldron of freshly caught trout, apologizing that she had nothing better. In northern Sweden the rivers and lakes squirm with trout and salmon trout, which are thus poor-man's food. So is most food judged by its quantity rather than by any standard of taste: the more it costs, the better it is; a herring and a pineapple change social status between London and Cape Town. My standards being British, I always salivated at these delicious fish.

Our hostess was talkative. She had never gone far from Ligga, but had a hungry interest in the world. London must be wonderful, all those finely dressed people in carriages; and America, too, if it weren't for the selling of women as slaves. That was a nasty business and should be stopped. Attempts at correction were snubbed; she had read about it and knew her world, and left us wondering whether her information came from novels or Communist propaganda. She had thought sometimes of marrying a handsome young man, but had decided they were more trouble than they were worth. She would sooner do her own work, for then she knew it was done well.

Ligga was memorable also for its well. So deep was it that the bottom could not be seen and a pebble's terse, hollow plop came up seconds after the pebble had left the top. The best part of half an hour was needed to water the horses. Water-mains being as rare in the forests as skyscrapers, all *bruks* have their well; the shaft sides are craggy with ice, and the water comes up cold and clear.

In some of the shallower wells the bucket is let down on the end of a rod which is fastened to a long beam pivoted upon a post; to the other end of the beam is fixed a lump of iron to balance the filled bucket as it is drawn up. Once or twice these tall beams told us of a *bruk* that we might otherwise have missed; there was all the welcome of an inn sign in these fingers pointing gauntly at the sky.

In time we came to feel that we were a party not of two persons but of four. Musti and Pilkis began to take on certain human characteristics; no doubt they had partly been there before and only with time did we see them, but also partly did they develop due to our constant contact. (Also no doubt did we take on certain equine characteristics, to our great benefit.)

Because of similar needs, all four minds were often filled

with similar thoughts: on waking, breakfast was the first, mingled with a usually private summing-up of the night's bedding—soft or hard, warm or cold; then upon the way we liked or disliked the weather and the country, as we bent our heads against the driving snow or bitter wind or rain, or relaxed in the sun. A grassy track was pleasure, a hard road sometimes tedium, a deep snowdrift a curse. Often we speculated upon the coming night's stable and fodder, hoping for the best but fearing the worst, with perhaps a lingering satisfaction from a good breakfast and a usually vain hope that a midday meal might come our fortunate way. To come towards evening upon a *bruk*, its bold redness beckoning from the forest's green, quickened the horses' stride without our prompting, for by this time all our thoughts were of food. And it was just as certain, should it be past nine o'clock and our searching eyes see no signs of habitation, that we were a grumbling company.

As with our thoughts, so often with our habits. We ate and travelled and rested together. We drank from the same becks, at the same time. (In the Interest of Hygiene I hasten to state that we scrupulously drank upstream from the horses, who did not seem to mind.) And, supremely proving our unity, when the cold or frequent drinking from the becks caused G.S. and me to halt upon the way, the horses felt a similar need and gruntingly joined in. In this way, as in most, there was the coherence of the perfect team.

Yet each horse had its private and distinctive habit, a part of its personality. Musti had to be amused, like a man who always takes a pack of cards upon a railway journey or cannot stay at home without a television set. He would not be long upon the way before boredom took hold of him. He fidgeted for entertainment. And that meant nibbling, preferably at a rump. It might be Pilkis's, or mine, or G.S.'s should he be leading him. He began softly with his lips and almost affectionately. But soon he sought more boisterous amusement. Suddenly inspired, he would nip sharply and in the same movement rear back from the rightly expected cuff on the nose from G.S. or myself or the squeal and flashing hoof from Pilkis, his eyes rebelliously aware of indiscretion. Then he would settle down for a while in perplexed resignation and look hurt.

Pilkis's particular foible was rolling on growing potatoes. Should she be left loose on a *bruk* for a little browsing, she would sooner or later search for the potato patch. And when she found it, she was enchanted. She pawed at them with a hoof to convince herself of her good fortune; and then, slowly as if revelling in anticipation, bent her legs beneath her and rolled happily onto her back and kicked and wriggled in delight. But it was an embarrassing habit for us and, once it was known, had to be guarded against. So much did these habits belong to their owners that none of the other three dared imitation; to have done so would have been an infringement of copyright.

In one other important way our habits differed. G.S. and I smoked tobacco; the horses' taste was for chewing it. The comparative cheapness of tobacco (we smoked the cheapest), the old groom's tale that it keeps horses clear of worms, and the benevolence of a sunny day sometimes stirred us to parting with a precious plug. To gather up the final taste Musti threw up his head and grossly curled and agitated his upper lip, while the feminine Pilkis merely licked her lips like a lady.

We held tobacco in deep respect. Cold, hunger, lack of bed or sleep could be and were joked about, but lack of tobacco never. Not that we found ourselves without it more than once or twice, for we were always careful to keep our pockets stuffed with a cherished reserve should we be starting on a long or dubious stage where the finding of habitation was doubtful. Every occasion demanded a filling of pipes. They consoled in misfortune, calmed in exhilaration, treating the one philosophically, turning the other into that complacency which, however smug in others, is most pleasing in oneself.

Should we unhappily find that there was no food for us tonight (and perhaps tomorrow morning as well); should we find at ten in the evening that we had lost our way or that the forest stood round us with no sign of habitation where we had expected it; or, as happened further south, should we have narrowly missed ignominious slaughter by a corner-cutting and speeding motor car, then solemnly and together out came the pipes from one deep pocket, a tin or a crumpled packet from another. And just as much the lesser occasions demanded the wisdom of tobacco: the thoughtful, the conversational, the argumentative, or merely to pass the time on the long treks through the forests or over mountain and bog.

If not the motive power of the expedition, it was at least the lubricant that saw to its smooth running. Salvation Yeo spoke wisely when he said:

Ah sir, no lie, but a blessed truth, as I can tell, who have ere now gone in the strength of this weed three days and nights without eating; and therefore, sir, the Indians always carry it with them on their war-parties: and no wonder; for when all things were made none was made better than this; to be a lone man's companion, a batchelor's friend, a hungry man's food, a sad man's cordial, a wakeful man's sleep, and a chilly man's fire, sir; while for staunching of wounds, purging of rheum and settling of the stomach, there's no herb like unto it under the canopy of heaven.

G.S. had been a cigarette-smoker, but had rightly judged the effete and characterless tubes to be insufficient for this open-air life. He bought a chubby pipe, shaped like the outlet pipe from a wash-basin and superbly crowned with a silver lid. Such a sturdy pipe was not easily broken when dropped from the saddle or otherwise ill-treated and had no long stem to gouge at him disquietingly from his trousers pocket when he was mounted. Its curves lay comfortably upon his embryonic beard, and with the lid clamped down, it burnt happily through the most annihilating snowstorm. My own, conventionally shaped and gadgetless, was but a poor affair. This unequal distribution of wealth caused me much communistic envy until in time I got possession of the pipe and veered sharply to the Right.

Surprisingly, and in contrast, we became almost indifferent to ale. We had thought that this life with its often enforced abstinence would sharpen our thirst. Perhaps the austerity of the Swedish bar and the poverty of the beer (except Norwegian Export) were partly to blame. But after serious discussion (we were worried lest the snow had blown into our wits) we concluded that in the case of the moderate and steady drinker, as distinct from the addict, a taste for ale is largely a mental one: a desire for company and conversation and an escape from ordinariness. Now we were doing something that meant a great deal to us, something that we felt to be worth while, so there was no feeling of futility in our living. Of course we had a drink from time to time when it offered, but we would have been no less content without it. From curiosity I tried schnapps, the traditional Scandinavian drink: truly it is Bacchus' brew, warming and enough to make a prioress prance. It would have been of great comfort to us in the Lapland blizzard and later during some sodden nights in the western marshes; but there, alas, was only an empty flask with its lingering bouquet of brandy.

Gradually our way of living became the most natural thing in the world to us as though of course everyone went each day on his horse from one place to another. No longer did it seem adventurous or eccentric or even unusual. Probably this meant simply that we had become nomadic. This, I think, is neither a very good thing nor a very bad one, for the praises of the vagabond's life are often romantically over-sung; on the other hand, the stationary rarely do more good and sometimes more harm. The virtue belongs to the natural or "simple" way of life, nomadic or settled, that for the most part takes thankfully from Nature without question or attempt at improvement, rather than committing "Civilization's" great and elementary mistake of trying to teach and coerce Nature as though she were a fool. As well might a mouse try to bully a lion: sometimes the instinct of the animal is wiser than the reason of man.

We soon learnt that the one thing to expect was the unexpected. Sometimes as we rode we said: "We'll get to this *bruk* or that village tonight—be good to have a feed and a bed." And as likely as not we would spend a shivering night without supper and with fir branches as a mattress. At other times we would say: "It's going to be a bad night; there's no habitation for miles and it's snowing like the devil," and amazingly we would as often as not come to a newly built charcoal-burner's hut or a lumberjack's shack, and sleep full of reindeer meat and potatoes by a great fire while the horses ate their heads off in a stable. The most primitive dwelling in the forest had its stable; here horses are the haulers of timber, for the unadaptable tractor would sink absurdly to its hubs in the drifts and the bogs. These unexpected places were always the most welcome.

We have never known such luxury as some of the barns provided. After a long stage in driving snow and a piercing wind to burrow at last into a stack of sweet hay, our bellies poulticed by a warm meal, was supreme bliss. Buried deep in the warming hay with only a nose left outside to breathe the cold, crystal air that whistled in from the forest gave a warmth combined with invigoration that no bedroom closed against the cold could give.

These moments were so delicious that we often resisted sleep for a while, talking slowly and contentedly and benevolently where two hours before we had perhaps argued each other's heads off, till from one there was suddenly no reply. Then—futilely, but comfortingly, to the speaker—he droned "Good night," turned slowly over, and, taking in a deep breath that came out in a long, contented sigh, fell asleep. Outside, the Arctic-born wind hurled its snow against the shaking pines.

10. Farewell Arctic

There is no love sincerer than the love of food. SHAW

AS we came near to Jokkmokk, there blossomed against its plain browns and yellows a posy of bright colours that we soon saw was the Danish and British flags reaching out flat and strong in welcome from the *gästis*.[1] In a foreign land we are both nationalists, and inside us we burst like barncocks to see our flags bold in these northern forests. Yet in the detachment of an English armchair I admit that the Scandinavian flags, all of them strong, simple crosses, have a beauty lacking in the complicated Union Jack: Sweden's in particular, taking its colours from sun and sky, flies gallantly against the deep greens of the forest. It seems a pity that the historic Cross of St. George is now so seldom seen above England.

That night we were feasted by the landlord of the *gästis* in his pseudo-barbaric beer-cellar—stone-walled, be-barrelled, and overshadowed by a great stuffed eagle that glared down

---

[1] Swedish inn.

upon us piercingly. Early morning saw toasts going berserk, our wolves increasing like rabbits, and our everyday blizzard blowing up enough to blast Lapland into the Arctic Ocean. But breakfast served reason, for we knew that this welcome spoke well not of ourselves but of Scandinavian generosity.

Both G.S. and I like our food. Perhaps my appetite was even keener than his because he had come from a wise and cultured little country that uses every inch of itself to grow food and whose inhabitants think more of this necessity than of petrol and television. Heavy eating in the past six years had been a more frequent achievement for him.

The evening meal, the *smörgåsbord,* in a Swedish *gästis* is ideally designed for the frustrated gourmand: on entering the little dining-room you find the usual small and personal eating-tables dominated by a larger one in the centre. This is heavy with hospitality: cold meats, smoked and pickled fish, eggs, cheese, Swedish breads, salads, sausages, sauces, and yoghurt. Should you have travelled for several days on only a couple of really good meals, you will, as we did, fix searching eyes upon the spread, drawn to it in determined steps. You will be as dangerous to interference as a bull-mastiff with a sirloin. You will take up knife, fork, and plate (the largest) and, starting at the nearest point, you will harvest your way around the table. Soon your plate is laden. A glance chooses for you a table as modestly placed as possible, in a corner. Then comes the silence of the conscientious worker. Very soon there is another visit to the central table—and another. By this time your gentlemanly modesty has a chance to assert itself and you force yourself to a slower pace of assumed indifference, dallying dishonestly with the serving-spoons, aware at last of the wondering glances of fellow eaters. Further visits, should they be possible, become even apologetic. To say "if possible" casts no slur on your abilities. But round about the fourth foraging will probably come the serving-maid—hastily, with the hot dish. This hints politely but plainly that you have already had your money's worth and probably far more; so you give up your plate and take your hot dish and coffee. As you leave the room, empty of its trifling and short-distance diners, you may, if you are shameless, slide a slice of ham and a piece of bread into your pocket against a doubtful future.

After such a meal we glowed with good-nature. We loved Sweden; we loved the inn; we loved the serving-maid. And after half an hour of lying in easy-chairs, whence we beamed more and more sleepily, we climbed to our rooms, took off our boots, rolled carefully onto our beds, opened our jackets, undid belts and the two top buttons, folded hands complacently upon bulbous bellies, sighed contentedly, and slept. . . . Later the moon might crane his neck over the quiet, cold forests, peering his well-fed face in the window to wake our snoring slumber. We should undress, put back our shirts, nod to him amiably, get into bed, and this time sleep till morning.

We rested in Jokkmokk for a couple of days, finding the village colourless, yet held by our host and his processional meals. But the journey called us and we saddled once more and went away to the south. Eight kilometres from Jokk-mokk, on a stretch of road by a lonely lake, we came to a signpost stating simply in four languages: "Polar Circle." Inevitably our thoughts flew westward over forest and mountain to another solitary sign, the pylon we had passed on the Norwegian coast, another paltry piece of metal marking another entrance to the North.

It seemed that today was eventful. Police came out from Jokkmokk to see us on our way; there was the usual display of passports and questionings of our purpose. But perhaps, as G.S. drily suggested, they only doubted our intentions towards the Arctic Circle.

During the next few stages we saw here and there signs of felling of the forest: upon frozen rivers logs were stacked, waiting for the ice to melt beneath them and float them down to the saw-mills towards the coast. Next morning as we went along the road we saw a timber-pile ready for burning to charcoal. Till now we had seen only the burnt-out wreckage of a pile, so with our usual curiosity for ancient crafts we rode over to it and exchanged greetings with the burners. Fortunately they found us legitimate excuse for their stopping work, for not often did they see a traveller. While G.S. spoke with them and questioned them on their art, I went to the circular pile. Its height was double that of a man, its area at the base about that of a small house. The logs were mostly pine stripped of bark and branches; how many there were I could only guess: there were at least a couple of hundred around its wall, so there must have been several thousand altogether. The top was a foot deep in moss and sods—to keep out the air, G.S. discovered. He was a ferret for knowledge (I felt he would have made an excellent spy), and as we rode away he explained that to make charcoal the timber must burn almost without air, that the pile is lit at the center of the base through a gap afterwards blocked up, and that due to the lack of air the pile may be a couple of weeks in the burning.

At night we came to a lumber camp, a cluster of wooden cabins and stables in a forest clearing. G.S. spoke to a lumberjack and, after some one-sided talk, asked if there would be a chance of a bed here tonight. The lumberman said we should see the foreman, in that cabin over there, and walked away without interest. The foreman was equally indifferent, but offered a couple of wooden beds without mattress or covering in a bare cabin, and left without further word. We did not mind the poverty of the beds, for we were glad of the offer, but there was, if not hostility, then a lack of friendliness unusual in northern Swedes. This sullenness of the camp made us ill at ease, and, strangely, we felt angry that they had let their country down, for we had come to like Sweden and its people. There seemed no excuse for them, as we had long left the rightly suspicious frontier with its nostrils twitching for the smell of Communism. Later we heard that many of the lumbermen are themselves Communists, so no doubt we were to them imperialists and thus to be distrusted. In the morning neither smiles nor farewell waves cheered us on our way: there were only faces staring, expressionless, over shoulders.

But at Moskosel next night friendliness returned unbounded. As we rode into the village, people shouted to people and went from windows to come back with others. They came out into the street and wished us God-speed. It was heartening after the aridity of the lumber camp, but embarrassing, so we were glad to shut a stable door privately behind us and say as we fed the horses that it was a pity we couldn't even out friendliness a little. A Dane living in the village hurried to invite us to eat with him. We did: four fried eggs each and bottles of beer.

Any chance encounter by the way was an excuse for gossip and the gathering of knowledge. These meetings were the more interesting for their rarity, as usually we rode through the day with no company but the pines. So when two days from Moskosel we came upon a lonely charcoal-burner working among the debris of his pile, we reined in and spoke to him. Charcoal-burners are often regarded in Sweden as a primitive race apart, like gipsies, but with the natural good manners of many people who work in the wilds he showed no curiosity in our purpose but only friendliness as he leant upon his shovel by a propped-up riddle. Near by was a shack with a foot-square hole as window: here, he said, he lived while he felled his timber and built his pile, then went away to his home while the timber burned, and came back in a week or two to gather up his charcoal. Yes, he was quite content—why shouldn't he be? And as we counted the blessings that he probably had and the irritations that he probably had not, we could but agree with him.

Soon we came out onto the road as it ran south near to Arvidsjaur. The surface of roads in northern Sweden is a mixture of earth and gravel, and after the thaw has pocked and ridged the surface a monstrous yellow first-cousin of the bulldozer comes up from the south and clanks hideously along the road, slicing off its top layer and pushing it to the sides, where it makes good going for a horse. This road-riding was uneventful but for Pilkis's gymnastics at the rare approach of a vehicle. One coming towards her she could keep her eye on and it might be tolerated with no more than a cautious side-step, but one coming up behind was unknown and so suspect, and should it oafishly hoot as it came level, she felt drastic action was called for. In her fright she either broke at once into a gallop in an endeavour to keep ahead or jumped sideways into the forest. This was bewildering, for I never knew whether to prepare to hold her or to slacken the reins and bring my weight forward for the jump. Had she been more than half-schooled, her frolics would have been easier to control, but riding along tracks gives little opportunity for the teaching of dressage. Riding her inside Musti proved of little use. Because her fear was real, punishment would have been worse than useless and its expectation would have added to her distress. I hoped that time and familiarity would cure her; if not, she must be halted upon the coming of traffic and half turned so that she might see it, a long and tiresome process. Meanwhile, the best that could be done was to talk to her quietly but cheerfully, soothe her by stroking her neck, and keep my temper when I suddenly found my-self among the trees upon a now calm horse, with a weal from the whorl of pine-needles rising across my face. But I eased my feelings upon the hooters-just-behind with four-letter Anglo-Saxon words in a far-reaching voice from the forest. For me there was no repentance: drivers without con-sideration for animals upon the road are all the things I said they were.

11. We Take a Bath

When you sleep in your cloak there's no lodging to pay.
WHYTE-MELVILLE

WE rode incongruously into Arvidsjaur, for it was new and square and macadamed. Here for the first time we felt modern influence upon Sweden seeping up from the south. Wide-grinning, chromium-slashed automobiles slid smugly along polished roads, new flats glistened among an afterbirth of rubble that screamed for clothing of soil and trees. Milk bars existed.

But in Arvidsjaur was an hotel that had a bath. For long we had ticked off the days to this bath, and Arvidsjaur had meant to us not a gathering of buildings but a vast container of hot water; not since leaving the ship had we managed to have a bath, and our need was great. We descended upon the hotel.

Oh, the revelry of that bath! No advertisement effervesced more suds, spume, and spindrift; no Roman emperors sweltered hotter or wallowed deeper. Time after time I turned on the tap till the surface rose to the overflow and I floated like a basking shark, only a blowhole of a nose above water. How comfortable was the world from that bath! With hooked toes I slowly stirred my shirt and vest which soaked with me, contented that they would feel fresh and sweet upon me in the morning, if a trifle damp, and my nostrils would be freed again for the happy scents of Nature. But when I went out, Arvidsjaur's stagnant petrol fumes sent me back wondering whether, after all, I was better off.

Once again the police questioned us, after what seemed a scarcely decent interval. We wondered whether the Harsprønget episode had come to official ears and set them flapping, and as I remember this in writing of it, I still wonder. Though in the near future we were to meet bigger and better spy-trouble, we did not know whether we raised it afresh from time to time, or whether it had gone before us from Hammerfest and kept its eye upon us along the route.

But there was a pleasant side to our stay in Arvidsjaur. Our good friends in Vittangi had sent us with introductions to an artist and his wife. They entertained us well in the informal fashion of artistic people, which has the virtue of putting a stranger at his ease immediately. They gave us a key, they showed us where food and drink were kept, they demanded only one thing: that we make ourselves at home. Yet after two days' stay we left Arvidsjaur without sorrow. Now we went no longer to the south but to the west, the marshes and the mountains, back into the remoteness of northern Sweden: to go south now would lead us into an increasing development, towards the crescendo of Stockholm. The peace of the forests had adjusted us to their wild, slow tempo; no longer were they claustrophobic, but pleasantly intimate. So on a rise in the road we turned in the saddles and looked back upon the town with satisfaction, forgiving it because we left it. Then we turned again to the forest and were content. That night we bivouacked in the friendly forest, for the first time from choice rather than necessity.

The second night brought good promise of the future. We had ridden to a *bruk* by a frozen lake; the peasant came out and pushed the horses and us into a well-built wooden stable and brought hay and a bucket of fat oats and a sack of pine-scented sawdust for bedding. Then he showed us to a little two-roomed house that stood by the shore of the lake. In it were a stove, a table, and two roomy beds. He hurried away and came back with a great hunk of ham, half a dozen eggs, goat's-milk cheese, butter, and a loaf of bread, thrust them upon us, and sat upon a bed, bursting with pleasure at our appreciation. He was a Norwegian who had escaped from the Nazis during the war and come over the Kiolen by himself and in the middle of winter to the sanctuary of Sweden. He had had no compass, no map, no skis, and had had to avoid any track, at least till he was over the border. The *fjells* had been metres deep in snow, the temperature at four or five thousand feet too low even to think of in comfort. Cook's *Scandinavia* (1939) describes the Kiolen area thus:

In the topographical sense Norway does not seem to have any natural frontier on the east side, and the familiar statement of our text-books about the great mountain ridge of Kiolen forming the boundary between Norway and Sweden is only a fiction, as no such definite boundary-line exists between Norway and her neighbours on the land side. Nevertheless a boundary does exist which is more effectual than mountains or rivers. Between Norway and her neighbours in the east stretches a wide area so utterly desolate and apart from the continuous area of human habitation that the greater part of it north of Trondheim was quite unknown up to the last century.

Certainly his was a considerable trek.

The following evening we climbed up a track into a grey wilderness, the ash-pan of a wide forest fire. Aptly, the sky was clouded in that flat greyness typical of an English winter's day, so that all was as though we looked upon a photograph. As far as we could see around us, trees had fallen twisted upon the ground, others still stood precariously, broken jaggedly like fractured bone or in the grotesque postures of rotting scarecrows, gaunt limbs shredded and dangling, streaked in black and grey and white. Once we passed a great eagle hunched motionless upon a stump. Soon a bitter, nagging wind came up to dry the grey dust and throw it up at us as it was loosened by the horses' hoofs, till the touch of colour upon us lost its difference beneath the dust and merged into the greyness. It was such a scene as might one day greet a primitive people ignored in war because of their poverty, coming wonderingly into a continent once blasted by a supreme nuclear bomb.

Our military map had shown a dwelling in the forest where we had hoped for food and shelter, but we could not expect to find it now. So when near midnight the horses began to slow their strides and droop their heads and there was still the dead forest and fifteen miles to Sorsele, we tied the horses to stumps so that they might at least rest, for they would find no foraging here. We lit a fire of heat-toughened timber. It was a comfortless place, in the half-dark of a Northern spring night, with the fire's light flickering weirdly upon grey stumps and lying logs as though we had encamped in a graveyard. So about five o'clock we saddled and rode, cold and grey, upon the way to Sorsele.

This was the last village of any size upon our route until we crossed into Norway. Here we stayed for a day to re-equip. Saddlery needed repairs. The horses' shoe-nails needed knocking home and re-clinching. Both horses and riders should eat much. We tried, without success, to buy films. We wrote letters.

We had planned to go south by the road to Storuman and then turn northwest towards Tärna, which lies by the foot-hills of the Kiolen. But we heard there was a good track going westward from Sorsele as far as a settlement of three *bruks* called Abacka. Beyond was a wilderness of marsh, but if we could cross it to a little village called Abborrberg, there

was another track that would take us on to the road to Tärna
so that we should go along one side of a triangle rather than
two and save about forty miles. The temptation of the short
cut is great and we gave way to it. Two or three miles from
Sorsele the track halts abruptly upon the bank of the broad
Vindelelv. A little one-man ferry large enough to take a
horse and cart joined the track with its continuation from the
opposite bank. As we rode down to the wooden landing the
ferryman was sitting upon a box on the stony shore. He was
surprised by us, but glad of company: no one had come here
for two days, he said, and he might better have stayed indoors
—and nodded towards a red house upon the bank.

We were full of doubt about the horses' reception of the
ferry, for it was probably a new experience for them and
what horror they might see in it we did not know. They
went on board quietly enough and we took off their saddles and reins, leaving only the bridle head-piece and the bit.
Thus we had firm control and they would have freedom to
swim in the unlikely event of their taking fright and going
overboard despite our hold upon the bits. We held them face
to face and, as the ferry moved from the shore carefully at
our request, fed them with sugar bought for the purpose in
Sorsele. We stood one each side of their heads to partly block
out their sight of the moving water while they spent the passage in a jealous and competitive interest in the sugar, for
nothing takes a horse's mind from unpleasant things better
than his belly.

This was an area of small lakes stippling the landscape like speckles on a trout's back. Thus, the track twisted to this side and that in continual evasion, but brought us in the evening to a friendly *bruk*. Here I entertained the little girl of the house by reading to her from her primer, my obtuse and halting pronunciation tickling her to laughter and delighting her to find that she could read better than a grown-up: no longer was she the least literate person in the house. In her eyes, at least, our night's lodging was well earned.

Next day we came to Abacka by a tree-fringed lake. This was not one of the good places: the peasants were doubtful of us; the horses shared a great draughty barn; and the best place we could find for sleeping was a stack of peculiar thistle-like hay that proved to be without warmth. We bought a packet of yellow powder called pancake mixture at one of the *bruks* that traded in a few groceries for the benefit of the others. This powder we mixed with water from the lake and cooked in a borrowed pan over a brushwood fire. The resulting paste would have repulsed any stomachs but those made ravenous by effort in the open air and by missing a meal. But the good St. Hubert had a way of compensating for poor quarters by a nocturne of Nature: there was a warmth and stillness in the air, and a bright orange sunset lit up the pines across the lake; soon the sun settled down upon the hills in the west, glowing upon the sky and emphasizing the dark ribbon of timber-traps that threaded the smooth roseate silk of the lake. "Spring is here," we said, and went back contentedly to the unfriendly hay.

12. Held by the Marshes

The most curious part of the thing was, that the trees and the other things round them never changed their places at all: however fast they went, they never seemed to pass anything. . . . Alice looked round her in great surprise. "Why, I do believe we've been under this tree the whole time! Everything's just as it was!" LEWIS CARROLL

WE left Abacka hungry but hopeful. "Tonight," we said, "we'll come to Abborrberg and there we'll eat our heads off." We had learnt that traveller's hunger has its blessings.

Abborrberg lay due west. A track went out from Abacka for some four miles to a *saeter*; thence a chain of three lakes and their connecting rivers stretched out to Abborrberg; to the north and parallel to the lakes was a range of *fjells*. We planned, therefore, to find our way along the flat land between them. As theoretical map work this was good: the water contained us on the left, the *fjells* on the right; all we had to do was to keep to the wide lane of forest between— and it would bring us out to Abborrberg. We rode confidently along the track.

Upon the shores of the first lake it faded like a spent wave in the lank grass of the *saeter*. We turned into the jumbled trees of the northern shore, riding away from it from time to time for easier going, yet always returning to the guiding lake.

At first all went comfortably and according to plan, until gradually and at first imperceptibly the going worsened, becoming piled with boulders and fenced by thick undergrowth that all the while drove us from the lake and slowed progress. So when we rested for a few minutes in a bald patch of the forest, we said: "It looks as though it'll be late when we get to Abborrberg and food. But probably it's better past this next lot of boulders." Yet always the way worsened: each time we were driven from the lake, the way back was harder. Often the horses stumbled, worrying us lest they sprain a tendon. We dismounted and led them.

In the late afternoon a massed wall of boulders and fallen trees came and stood across our path. G.S. held the horses while I scrambled down to the shore, but even by the water's edge the rocks plunged out among floes laden with their cargo of dirty, melting snow. We must go into the *fjells* and hope to find a way along their sides.

So we climbed upward and still the west was barred. How far or how high we went I cannot tell, but soon soft snowdrifts came sprawling between the feet of pines, clutching at us to the knees. Slowly we came out above the forest onto a high tundra where the sun had melted the snow, and at last the west was open again.

12. *Held by the Marshes*

The light Northern night and the intensity of our efforts had smothered time, so when G.S. looked at his watch it was at first with disbelief: midnight had come and gone. We would bivouac; and then, we said, we'll arrive in Abborrberg in good time tomorrow and we can have a good rest after we've eaten—and speculated upon the meal's contents.

We looked round for food for the horses, finding only a patch of poor reedy grass that might at least ease the emptiness of their bellies; here we unsaddled and turned them loose. We laid out the groundsheets one upon the other, heaped the saddlery in one corner, and tossed for first sleep. G.S. won, squirmed into the sleeping-bags, pulled his minute pillow beneath his head, and slept.

To help pass the long hours of watching as well as for warmth, I gathered brushwood and dead branches, and soon there was the comfort of a fire. I crouched over it cross-legged and smoked, from time to time herding the horses when they strayed in search of better food. Soon they tired both of search and poor grass and gathered round the fire to blink sleepily in its warmth and start at the louder crackles.

When I woke G.S. at the end of my watch, we discussed plans for the day. Below and perhaps five miles away was a stretch of water—probably, we said, the second of the lakes. We would start early in the morning and make for its far end. Then I wriggled into the sleeping-bags and slept.

Almost at once, it seemed, G.S. woke me. "It's five! I suppose we'd better be going." I agreed—hypocritically, for I had not the slightest wish to do anything but sleep.

There was no sun to guide us, but believing this was the second lake that we saw, we could find roughly the direction of Abborrberg from the map. The going was fair, like moorland underfoot with small berry bushes and clumps of brushwood. Normally we should have ridden, but the horses had neither slept nor fed, so sadly we walked. Soon we came into awkward ground once more, rough and wet and laced with the bleached and brittle branches of fallen trees. For a long time we plodded through this dreary scene, always going down and towards Abborrberg. Now and then a peak like the crown of a bowler hat stood up between the trees, yet many miles away; from what we had heard of its shape in Abacka, this would be the Abborrberg *fjell,* and at its foot was food. We thought and talked of food as hungry men will, beginning with the good filling stuff of the *bruk* that we expected soon and working up through the whole scale of gastronomy to favourite exotic delicacies, till we drooled ungracefully upon our beards and some new difficulties of passage filled our thoughts. For now we came to forest and belts of snow once more, soft and treacherous snow, the winter's deep drifts barely lessened by the thaw, hiding fallen trees, rocks, and holes, often supporting us but giving treacherously beneath the horses' weight. Once or twice the sudden unexpected jolt brought them to their knees till they scrambled out with snorts and frightened eyes and followed us once more in resignation.

At last the segments of a grey band of water appeared between the trees. This would be the round-shaped lake that we had hoped to find, which we must pass to the north to avoid the river that emptied from its southern shore to the second of the big lakes. From its northern shore we believed we could travel west to Abborrberg. But when we had pushed between the trees and clinging undergrowth to its shore we saw that this was a long-shaped lake uncharted upon the map, and above its far end the Abborrberg *fjell* rose still many miles away. This was unfortunate, but not the worst. As we thrust through undergrowth and deepening snow-drifts a sound of rushing water that had started faintly now grew louder, till suddenly we came out to a sweeping torrent swollen by melting snow and emptying into the lake. It seemed almost certain that it came down from the range of *fjells* where we had spent the night. I cut a stick and plunged it deep into the torrent to try its depth, but before it touched bottom it was wrenched away by the torrent's force. Obviously neither horse nor man could keep his feet against it; it was another barrier between us and Abborrberg. We might try going to the south of the lake, but another river would empty from it into one of the three big lakes or their connecting rivers. The only way was to follow the river and look out for a possible crossing-place.

The going was poor, still with deep drifts and fallen trees that pushed us repeatedly away from the bank. But the river at last turned towards the west, and in renewed hope we followed it. It was foolish optimism. For now we came to worse than the drifts, the fallen trees, or even the turgid river; these were bad enough, for they hemmed you in and lost your direction and forced you to unbelievable twists and turns so that you must go five miles to progress one, but they were serious only because they tired you. Now we came into marsh. It was not the sort where water lay and your feet sank a couple of inches and then trod firmly, but the slow-sucking bottomless kind. We stepped into it suddenly: one moment we had gone upon firm ground, the next my feet sank beneath me as though I were going down in a slow-moving lift. All in a moment, and by instinct I shouted to G.S. to stop, fell flat on my back on the solid ground behind, and snatched viciously on Pilkis's bridle to catch her in the mouth and so jerk her backwards; her eyes goggled at this unexpected assault. The holes made by my feet filled at once with muddy water, where bubbles rose and broke, letting loose a stench suggestive of decayed cabbage. Time after time we tried to find ground that would hold us and let us go forward; each time the sticks with which we now tried our way sank squelching and without resistance into the slime and we jerked on the bridles. The morass sprawled like a giant octopus throwing out tentacles that never loosen once they hold, and it seemed that we had gone in between two of them and must return the way we had come. Once or twice we probed towards the north, only to withdraw again. A few times a stretch of low bushes promised firmer going but they died away in the marsh. Once we made good progress along the firm bed of a stream till it broadened out into flood-water lying across a morass and the ground sagged beneath us again and sent us back down the hurrying stream.

12. *Held by the Marshes*

Sometimes we came out on open ground that disclosed the Abborrberg peak and confirmed direction, but most of the time we went through the blinding forest, and here too was marsh beneath the snowdrifts and the fallen trees. Often low-hanging branches or crowding trunks snatched at the saddles, sometimes slowing the horses in their tracks. The saddle-girths were leather and strong, but the wallets were torn from their straps and dangled foolishly from the pommels. Now and then the horses, in their hunger, snatched at little bushes of the blueberry type and we paused to let them fill their mouths.

Some time after noon we were probing doubtful ground, looking down for the warning orange or verdigris of moss or the thinly spaced grass sprouting from sludge, when in disbelief I saw a hoofmark—and another—and then more. A horse had gone here and not long since. Where another horse could go, ours could; this would be a peasant's horse, and he would know where he was going. I shouted to G.S., and we bent over the trail as though we had struck gold. But when we looked up to follow its direction, a familiarity in the pattern of forest and marsh struck us. G.S. spoke flatly for both of us: "That's Musti's hoofmark; we've been here before, a couple of hours ago."

There was only one thing to do: to make into the *fjells* again, where there would be less marsh.

I remember little of incident in the next six hours, only a repetition of advance and retreat, the coming to the oozing moss of morasses and drawing back and trying another way, the treacherous snowdrifts and clutching trees and going into forest and coming out upon open marsh, and rising hope crushed by disappointment. I thought of a ballet I had once seen where the ballerina, trapped in a circle of devils, twisted and turned this way and that in futile effort to escape. It was pitiful to see the horses, almost dragged along by the reins in their weariness, their pathetic eyes accusing us of wantonness.

All day there had been no sign of life but for a pair of ravens that once circled croaking down towards us in curiosity. It was as if the whole world had turned to marsh and we were the only people upon it. But at last, as the dimming of light that was night came down upon us almost unnoticed, we found we were on the slopes of the *fjells* and the marshes were less frequent. Yet it seemed that every obstacle of Nature had combined to block our way to Abborrberg. We came out of the forest to the banks of a beck, probably the one that had balked us in the morning, and, though here it was narrower, yet its banks dropped vertically to a boulder-strewn bed. The beck was still swift and powerful, though not enough to sweep the horses from their feet and it would have reached no higher than their bellies; but the sudden drop from bank to bed, onto piled boulders treacherously hidden by the swirling water, would almost certainly have lamed them if not broken a leg. We searched upstream and down, but the sudden bank was unbroken.

We were tired now. We must rest ourselves and the horses for a while before we could go on, for we had not halted all day. The first day we had gone seventeen hours; yesterday (for it was already morning) we had gone twenty. At only two miles an hour that was over seventy miles, and on ground about as bad as it could be. Already we had been two days and nights without eating and had slept only two hours since leaving Abacka. We could not go that far again today, and even with a few hours' sleep we must face a rapid fall in strength. The horses, too, must rest and sleep even if they could not eat.

Upon a mound crowned by a cluster of firs we unsaddled them and left them loose to pick at dry and stunted bushes. They toyed with them and dribbled out the residue uninterestedly. It had now turned cold, a dank, penetrating cold coming up from the saturated swamp. With relaxation the water in our boots chilled us and we shook. The scramble of the last two days had half torn the soles from G.S.'s boots, so that the cold water flushed in and out of them as an efficient cooling-system, whereas in mine it stayed and was tempered by the warmth from my feet. His knees actually knocked together. We broke dead branches from the trees and with shaking hands piled up a fire, gathering round it with the horses and cowering with cold. It was fortunate that we had stocked with matches and tobacco before leaving Abacka, for without a fire there would have been little comfort in these swamps. The wish for food had left us and tobacco had settled our stomachs' needs; again I thought of Salvation Yeo's testimony to tobacco—"who have ere now gone in the strength of this weed three days and nights without eating . . . for when all things were made none was made better than this . . . to be a hungry man's food, . . . a wakeful man's sleep, and a chilly man's fire"—and I felt that, however badly St. Hubert had neglected us these past two days, at least he had been with us at Abacka, and that we could not blame him for being a bit chary of these swamps.

Tonight we must both sleep, for time was running out and could not be spent in watching. We picketed the horses by the fire and spread out one groundsheet, laying the sleeping-bags upon it and covering them with the other groundsheet. The Abborrberg peak, still several miles away but seeming nearer now, stood out sharply before the early-rising sun, and in accordance with our habit of photographing milestones in the journey, I took out my camera to record it. Yet not until the photograph had been printed months later did I see the threat in black and gathering clouds. Before I slept I decided to make for the peak in the morning, hoping to cross the beck where it surged between boulders and bring from Abborrberg food and a guide who knew the marshes.

I half woke, shivering again, to feel rain falling lightly on my face. Perhaps it did not matter very much, but so far our bodies had kept dry and there might be something I could do to keep them so. I dragged myself from half-sleep and quietly, without disturbing G.S., raised myself upon an elbow. Then I saw that this was not rain: it was snow. In sudden fear I looked between the firs in the direction of Abborrberg, and for the first time all hope went. A silent-falling white curtain cut us off from the world. There was no peak any more.

Slowly and silently the snow settled down upon the groundsheet, already a thin white quilt. G.S.'s hair and beard were white as an old man's, showing strangely against his face, which glistened like a new-washed schoolboy's with melted snow. The gaunt pines, the ugly marsh, everything but the dirty ashes of the fire were covered by the beauty and purity of fresh-fallen snow, mocking our misfortune.

Ill-luck had been so much with us that I was quietly fatalistic. The snow was there; if it stopped, we should see the peak; if it went on for days, as it might, we should not. Then whether we went or stayed would make little difference: a quarter of a mile from the camp we should have no more idea of direction than a man in a mountain mist. Yet with a wish to do anything that might be helpful, I got up quietly and went to the sodden, sizzling ashes and ridiculously turned our soaked boots upside down to keep out the snow. Then I went to the horses. They stood resignedly, half-dozing, with snow upon their backs and manes, but they were not shivering. No doubt they had stood out in worse than this, and not for the first time I was thankful for their hardy breeding. Nothing could be done for them. I patted their necks and spoke quietly to them, and went back to bed. It was almost comforting to feel that there was nothing else left to go wrong, and common sense told me the only wise thing to do was to sleep again. Now beyond all worry, I did so.

Yet when we woke about five hope came back once more. A sharp sun had risen upon us, eating away the snow and bringing back the Abborrberg peak, which glistened beneath its melting snow. We decided that we should both set out for Abborrberg, for two would have a better chance of getting there than one, and if one failed, the other might still succeed. We did not like to leave the horses, but our best chance was also theirs. We debated whether to picket them or leave them to search for what food they might. It was unpleasant to think that if we did not reach Abborrberg they might be fastened and slowly starve, but loose they would probably wander in their hunger and be sucked down horribly into a morass. Tethered, their chances were fairly good; loose, they were far worse. They drooped motionless in their resignation, our stirring giving them no hope of better things. We loosed them again to find what they might and led them to the beck for water, but they only dipped their muzzles in it, craving the warmth of food. Our kit we piled upon one groundsheet and covered it with the other, and leant the saddles against a tree by the sodden grime of last night's fire.

G.S. scribbled a note of our route upon a leaf of his diary and impaled it upon the spike of a dead branch, and as an afterthought I pulled the top groundsheet from the bundle and laid it light side uppermost where it could be seen from a low-flying plane. Should our disappearance be noticed and reported, a search from the air might be begun, and if our groundsheet was spotted, at least the position of the horses would be known. We tethered the horses again, and as we went, each of us looked back at them without speaking, wondering whether we should see them again.

The teeming beck held us up for a while till we found a crossing on boulders, ending by a jump at an overhanging branch. At last our luck had changed. The sun and our watches gave us direction in the forest. There were still the knee-deep drifts and unseen holes, but we could go upon bogs that would have given beneath the horses, and without them we went less slowly. At intervals we slashed a peel of bark from the trees so that on our return the white blazes would stand out against the massed dullness of trunks and mark our way. The going was still varied, so that we came out onto firm and snowless lanes between the trees until the drifts piled up again or a sudden giving of the ground halted us and turned us another way. But all the time Abborrberg was coming nearer.

Energy came in waves, forcing our legs till they suddenly rebelled and weakened so that we dragged, scarcely caring, until the will charged our legs again. Once G.S. said he must stop for a while, and sat upon a fallen trunk. I feared our dropping off to sleep in the soothing sun, but rest seemed necessary. There was a light-blue look of fatigue in his eyes. But I could have been in little better shape, for as we came out into an open space and again the mass of the Abborrberg peak stood up, now nearer, I saw two climbers sitting upon a rock at its summit. Elated, I pointed them out to G.S.; as I looked at them fixedly I saw one handing something to the other—food, perhaps. But G.S. could not agree: why should any climber be here in this wilderness and at this time of the year? It was not Scotland or Wales, and the peasants see no pleasure in climbing their *fjells* any more than the Londoner spends his Saturday afternoons in Westminster Abbey. We went on again and I realized that if these were people they must be twenty feet tall, for the peak was still some four miles away. I felt less sure of myself.

Now we continuously fought off sleep; time after time we weakened and for an instant tasted the ecstasy of drowsiness, our eyelids dropping to be prized open again by a jarring effort of will. It was like fighting against the last moments of drowning.

Once or twice when I could not lift the weight of my eyelids I pricked my wrist with the point of my knife to jolt myself awake; partly through sleepy lack of judgment and partly through anger at myself, I jabbed harder than necessary, so that there was a trickle of blood. I licked it, at first to stop its dripping on my clothes but soon because I found it pleasant and even stimulating: perhaps blood in small amounts has some of the properties of meat extract. I doubt whether in considerable hunger we are far from cannibalism.

About noon I was trudging dully a few yards in front of G.S.—and suddenly stopped. I strained my eyes and for an instant looked away, saying nothing, remembering the figures on the *fjell*. I looked again. Yes, there was a track such as we had often ridden upon, used by the peasants for driving cattle to the *saeters*. G.S. had come up, wondering at my sudden stopping, and when he saw the track his face lit with thankfulness. "Thank God for that," he said, and after looking up and down the track: "I think that's our way, to the right." It was good to hear him say so, for I had thought the same. We set off, quickened by hope and the easier going of the track that gradually turned towards Abborrberg. At last we saw a grey horizontal line cutting across the uprights of the trees: it was a roof—but of a house or a deserted barn on a *saeter*? We came nearer, and in a red wall was a window, and at the window a curtain. It was Abborrberg.

We came into a clearing over a little plank bridge, knocked at the door of the nearest house, and went in. A woman looked up, startled, from her cooking, and G.S. spoke to her slowly, leaning against the doorpost.

She brought us dishes of porridge and went out to find her husband. Soon he came in and G.S. told him of our difficulties and the horses' whereabouts and asked him if he could show us a way through the marshes. Doubtfully he answered: "No one goes there except on the *saeter* track until midsummer, when the marshes have dried up. But there is a man here in the village who knows tracks over the marshes. I'll see if I can find him." He got up and went out while we continued with the porridge. Soon he came back with a short, stocky man, broad-faced and with high cheekbones like a Lapp. Perhaps he was a half-breed and so more than half a nomad. He sat and stared at us stolidly and smoked a pipe while G.S. spoke with him. He did not speak until he had finished smoking; then he got up. "Come," he said, and went out.

We followed him along a track at the foot of the mountains. Food had cut one of the links of the chain that was holding us—long marches, no food, lack of sleep—and now we felt comparatively refreshed. Soon he turned and twisted into the marshes but always on firm going, quiet and confident. We came to the violent beck; he looked quickly up and down for some particular place, found it, and waded through. To our surprise, it came barely to our knees. Then at last in a familiar pattern of marsh we saw a clump of trees upon a mound. "He's found it, all right," I said unnecessarily, and shouted; there came a rapturous whinny and there was a sudden movement of yellow among the black and green of the trees.

In exultation and relief we patted the horses and spoke to them and put an arm round their necks, till a fear of seeming sentimental turned us with a practical air to gathering saddles and equipment. Soon there was a cavalcade winding its way through the forest and swamp: leading it, a man short and silent; then a man followed docilely by a black horse; and lastly, plodding in the steps of another man, a yellow horse.

Late that night a steady munching could be heard from a warm stable in Abborrberg, and from a peasant's dwelling the long breathing of two men deeply asleep. And when we woke, it was night again.

13. The Last Frontier

*There's not a nook within this solemn pass but were an
apt confessional.*   WORDSWORTH

TWO days' sleeping and eating can do a man (and a horse)
a lot of good. We had come into Abborrberg like stragglers
from a routed army, dirty, hollow-eyed men dragging heavy-
headed, shambling horses. We left well-fed on horses proud
as hackneys. G.S., the younger man, had recovered by the
first day; I, who had been less tired in the marshes, had felt
lethargic as if recovering from flu.

We found quarters that evening in the stables of a lumber
camp by a great, quiet lake. Massive trunks basked in shoals
by the shore, while a red motor boat pottered among them,
leaving a long-lasting, round-rippled wake to mark the
smoothness and throwing silence into relief by the hollow
chug of its slow-turning diesel engine. Yet because it stressed
the stillness by its frequent stopping and because of the mel-
lowness of its sound, it was not discordant.

We lit a fire upon the shore and cooked food pressed on us in Abborrberg, sitting against a stranded log and smoking long into the stillness of the night in the fire's red comfort. Around the shore firs reflected darkly in the polish of the lake.

At noon next day we were halted in a hollow of the forest, lying back half-dozing with hands behind our heads while the horses pulled at a patch of peeping spring grass. The air was soft with contentment. Suddenly Musti's head jerked up and bristled with attention, ears tense and nostrils wide, and in a moment he was gone into the forest, followed by Pilkis with her tail trailing high. We jumped up growling and followed them, but almost at once they were out of sight and we could only take the flattest and most open ways that, horse-like, they would be likely to choose. Now and then we were reassured by hoofmarks in soft ground, long-spaced and the toes digging lower than the heels, till we lost them for a while and had to return and choose another way. At last these occasional hoofmarks closed in and toes and heels were imprinted to equal depth, showing that the horses were now walking. When at length we saw them, it was in a sheltered hollow of green and juicy grass, where they gorged like truant schoolboys forgetful of their wrongdoing in a bag of sweets. Though we had followed them with breathless threats, the relief was such that we had to forgive them. What had startled them we never knew: wolves were not to be expected south of the Circle, though a bear it might have been or perhaps a wolverine.

We came unexpectedly to a decaying house by a lake, where close at hand grass grew upon a slope laid out to the sun. We peered into the caves of its rooms, the dust-dirty emptiness of all discarded buildings. We liked better the clean dust of hay, but here at least was shelter, and food for the horses. An unbolted door gave us entrance, and we searched with strange fastidiousness for a clean space to lay the groundsheets.

Two days later, approaching Tärna, we felt the nearness of the Kiolen. Where before they had been as clouds piled up on the horizon, a white half-rim to the earth, now they stood out as individuals. They made travel more satisfactory by showing us our immediate goal, holding it out as a carrot to a donkey and by their coming nearer giving us visible proof of progress such as we had not known in the forests, where had rarely been a measure of movement.

Tärna was a place of consequence on the journey. It was the last village in Sweden and so the last before we should cross the Kiolen. Here we could buy a meal; thus it was of the highest strategic importance, for the next place where food would be certain was Hattfjelldal in Norway, three days over the *fjells*. We ate to make up for the last few days since leaving Abborrberg, for they had been rather lean. Then we ate for today. Finally we ate for the next three days. I am certain the story of this orgy is still told in Tärna; that it has become a legend like some chronicled medieval feast.

We left Tärna stolid as suet dumplings on midsummer day, though secretly we had little confidence in misplaced humps, which experience had shown less lasting than the camel's. Soon we left the road that runs from Tärna, and turned away sharply to the west along a tight valley rising in the foothills of the Kiolen and squeezing a lake dappled with snow-piled floes. At Tärna the great lake had lapped against its new-thawed shores; now we climbed back into winter.

In the evening we came to a humble *bruk,* the furthermost pioneer into the mountains. Here would be our last stay in Sweden; tomorrow we should cross the frontier. The old peasant came out and gave us everything. For the horses, hay and corn and a primitive stable upon the side of a hill; as we settled the horses he puffed in with a couple of buckets of water that he had lugged up the cattle track chiselled in the hillside. And then, finding the cattle stalls cramping for the horses, he at once knocked down two boskins. A very few times in life you meet this man; his eyes tell you at once it is he, at peace with his conscience and so with the world. Back in his house we ate great platefuls of meal porridge from a well of an earthenware bowl. The peasant's old workhand, with a paunch like a planet bulging an inadequate waistcoat, came in unheralded and at ease. He joined us slowly and populated a chair. Between plates he leant slowly backward, blowing up further with a deep inhalation let out at last in a long and infinitely satisfied "YA"—and then "YO" and again "YA"—each time in a waft of well-being. He engulfed an ocean of porridge.

The next day was a milestone in the journey, for we were to come to Norway. A journey such as this is mentally split into sections, partly because to think of it as one is too much for the imagination and partly because it is satisfying to be able to tick off stretches of it as completed, for by this means you illicitly taste achievement many times before the final goal. Every day's end brought this satisfaction to some extent, but these sections were determined by geography rather than by time and were partly of our own choosing. The first had been the coming down to the Muonioelv from the Lapland plateau and the arrival in Sweden; the second, the long stage southward through the forests to Arvidsjaur; then the going westward to the Norwegian frontier and the coming to another country. Next would come the trek southward again on the way to Trondheim.

It was a satisfying day. We went over snow-covered tracks in treeless and frozen-lake-pitted country that reminded us of Lapland, halting from time to time to take the horses into becks for the good of their legs as was our custom, till we crossed the frontier and came for the night to the first Norwegian *bruk*. When we started next morning, the snows of the Kiolen were glittering in a brilliant sun, combining with the rare and alcoholic air to fill us with energy. On such a morning you cannot fail. When we rode side by side, we talked with unusual loquacity; when separate, each sang quietly and cheerfully to himself while drinking in the stupendous scene that piled up to the high pass before us, the *fjells* growing in height and grandeur and rising ever steeper till they almost closed together in the towering walls that hemmed in the pass. Up here all was rigid in the grip of cold; there was no sign of life but the claw-marked trail of a bear that had shambled across the track. The going became hard, and we had to keep a wary eye upon the snow masses heaped up upon the hanging crags for warning of an avalanche. Once we came to a great tumbled barrier of snow that had crashed a thousand feet from the crags above, and we ploughed deeply through it. Now a bitter wind tore up the pass, sweeping streamers of snow from the steep summits so that they recalled cooling-towers with their steam flattened out by the wind. We remembered reading in a Bergen paper of a man wanted for murder who had taken to the Kiolen with food, skis, and a rifle. There he had eluded ski patrols for weeks before he was at last cornered and, after shooting two of his pursuers, was himself shot dead. We felt that he had chosen his ground well. When at last we came to the top of the pass we stopped to rest the horses' heaving flanks. Behind, the track dropped into a great chasm; before us it wound as a long ribbon down through a vivid green valley that thrust up like a wedge into the whiteness. When we started again and rode down into the summer below, the horses were elated and strode out eagerly. Spring had come fitfully upon us in the lowland forests around Arvidsjaur and Sorsele, where the strengthening sun had melted the snow, yet since we had come into the slowly rising marshes and lately the foothills, we had ridden back into uncompromising winter and the rare spring grass had gone once more. Now we went down upon the green of spring between the white of winter to Hattfjelldal, a village in the foothills of the Kiolen. Its buildings were of unpainted wood instead of the bold red of northern Sweden, stressing that this was another country. Beside it was laid out a war-time German aerodrome now disused, its prim flatness seeming out of place among the mountains dominated by the Hattfjell, the "Hat Mountain," which gives its name to valley and village. The likeness to a hat recalled the Abborrberg peak, but that had been a bowler hat, while this was a top hat with flat crown and vertical sides.

There were letters for us, enclosing newspaper cuttings from Denmark and England. In Denmark we were described as "Polar Riders" (what a title for a strip cartoon!), while a British paper, on hearing of our staying with Lapps, printed as a heading "Wigwam Nights." This was superb. It gives one an idea for a glamour musical based on our escapade, perhaps with the sub-title "The Squeezing of the Squaw." It seemed that we started from Lapland thus: "With a gee-up, Brown started off the three horses across the tundra wastes. . . ." (It was not suggested we had a photo-finish when the time came to say "Whoa.") But all this kept us happy for the day and on many other occasions besides.

The horses' shoes had lasted well, being made of good Kiruna metal, but the rocks of the Kiolen had been hard on them, so that at the toes they had worn to the hoof. There was no blacksmith, but a farmer who shod the local horses agreed to do ours. So while one horse was shod, the other cropped the plentiful grass that rustled almost secretively in the sun, showing that at last we had come into summer.

14. Sudden Summer

For lo, the winter is past . . . the flowers appear on the earth; the time of the singing of birds is come. . . .

SOLOMON

THE summer was still a delicious novelty as we rode down from Hattfjelldal towards the green Svenningdal. Translucent birch leaves danced and rustled happily in the sun's beams that flickered through the trees to jostle our eyelids and warm newly bared arms and necks. Wild flowers flecked the wayside in a dozen vivid colours; between the trees shone lakes no longer white or mottled but rich blue in the sun, sapphires sparkling with silver. Behind us the snow masses of the Kiolen stood still stern in their winter, a reminder that on the last stage our Arctic jackets, now clinging unwanted across the saddle pommels before us, had wrapped welcome collars around our ears. Now from G.S.'s pocket drooped the shrunken fingers of fleece-lined gloves, old friends gratefully discarded. And up to us came the long-missed smell of warm horse.

That evening we came to a little village in a tree-clad val-ley. The post office was also a farm-house, and here we asked where we might find stabling. We were told in a hostile man-ner that there was no accommodation in this village and it would be better to move on. Used to warm friendliness, we were astonished. Was Norway, unlike Sweden, to be an un-friendly country? Or had we been spoilt by our previous wel-comes and come to except too much? We rode on, perplexed and saddened, till the winding road came out by a farm-house. Here we were luckier: we could stable the horses and sleep in the barn. This summer evening called us to sit out in the still-warm embers of the sun, so we led the horses on to the long grass around the barn and turned them loose. They would find no reason for straying from this plenty; indeed, they had no time for moving except to the uneaten grass be-fore their noses. We sat against a couple of rocks some yards apart and chatted. "This is a fine, carefree life," we said, "away from all troubles and man-made regulations." This was free-dom. So we watched with easy detachment a car pull up and disgorge its two occupants, and felt a self-satisfied pity for them that they missed so much. We smiled at them benignly as they came towards us; it was good to speak with friendly folk. They walked over to G.S., returning only shortly my suggestion that it was a beautiful evening. As my Norwegian was limited, I caught nothing of the conversation. At length G.S. got up and came across to me in indignation. "Police again. They want to know what we've taken on the cameras today. They had heard from Hattfjelldal that we were photographing the aerodome. One of them's going there in the car to find out more about it."

We argued with the remaining plain-clothes man. We were rightfully offended. We were Danish and English, and Norwegians had no better friends. Did he think we were Russian spies? He did not commit himself. When the other returned, they talked aside for a few moments—and when they had finished, we were under arrest. We were spies. We were to go to the jail at Mosjöen, forty miles to the north. But now we no longer burst with indignation, for it had dawned upon us that this arrest was not altogether a bad thing. They could hardly take us away before we had tended the horses, which would be well cared for at police command as well as at our request. The odds were against our being detained more than a couple of days at the most before we could give the police evidence that we were merely eccentric travellers and not teeth in the cogs of Moscow. We had run short of film in the long journey through the nearly uninhabited country of the swamps and *fjells,* and there was other shopping to be done. My only shirt was parting down the back and seemed a little untidy now that we often rode jacketless, and the skeletons of my last pair of socks called for replacement—had, indeed, been calling ever since the marshes. So, the horses fed and stabled, we took our saddlewallets under one arm (G.S., with habitual foresight, tucking his pillow smugly beneath the other) and seated ourselves in the car.

On arrival at the police station we were again questioned

XVII. *"Forests and belts of snow"*

XVIII. *On the way to Tärna*

XIX. *"Reminding us of Lapland"*

XX. *"We took them into becks for the good of their legs"*

XXI. *Carving of Troll's head*

XXII. *"Waiting for the winter's logs"*

XXIII. *Bridal saddle*

XXIV. *National costume*

xxv. *The long ways of the Dovre*

xxvi. *Gorm crosses a beck*

XXVII. *From the Jotunhei-men into "a flat and fertile valley"*

XXVIII. *Approaching Näroydal*

XXIX. *"The bridge swayed and sprang"*

XXX. *"Pilkis pricked suspicious ears"*

XXXI. *Unsaddle—for the last time*

XXXII. *Sculpture of G.S. and Musti in Copenhagen*

by the detectives. How many photographs had we taken to-day? G.S. said two, I said four. What of? We couldn't re-member, except that there was one of the Hattfjell. What was the reason for our journey? The best answer we could give them was the best we could give ourselves: that we liked it. Altogether, it was rather obscure and, we had to admit, not very satisfactory. They confiscated our cameras and would develop our films while we waited—in jail.

A uniformed policeman escorted us to the cells. From one a garrulous toss-pot abused the policeman, who replied that he would see him in the morning. He pushed a massive key in one of the doors and swung it open for us; he wished us good-night and clanged the door to behind us. We were en-tranced. Deep mattresses awaited us in a cream-distempered cell. Perhaps we should decently have felt dismay. But there was no reason for it. For the first and last time on the journey we had comfortable lodgings without either payment or the uncomfortable feeling that we owed for hospitality. It was indeed the supreme hospitality. Should there be a homicidal maniac at large somewhere in Scandinavia, then no one could be safer from him than us, for we had been given our own police protection; every wolf-pack in Lapland could come down and howl around our walls and leave us undisturbed. By the electric light we pulled the mattresses into the corner of our choice; G.S. smoothed out the pillow while I fashioned one of boots and jacket, as was my habit. We lay back with luxurious sighs, lit contented pipes, and cupped hands behind our heads. Except for Hattfjelldal, we had had no softer beds since leaving Sorsele. I became reminiscent. I assured G.S. that this was the very finest jail I had ever been in. Such comfort, such cleanliness, such civility. He scented a story and asked for it. I began. The time was September 1938, the place Johannesburg. Chamberlain had gone to Munich, but had not yet returned with his scrap of paper. War seemed imminent. There's no fool like a young fool, and George and I were both: we decided to go to England and join the Air Force. One afternoon we took our baggage to the station, got tickets for the midnight train to Cape Town, and settled down to neat brandy in the Victoria bar. By tea-time we felt aggressive. Now, in the city was a German club, a heavy stone building with the Nazi swastika flaunted from its flagmast. Good show! We would get that flag. But we were interrupted and, after a short and bloody fight, were thrown out. We picked ourselves up, agreed that this was but a temporary defeat, and cleared off down the street with the imposing doormat emblazoned *"Der Deutsche Klub."* Unfortunately, police had been watching the club, for feeling was high against the Germans. Whistles blew; we were surrounded and arrested. At the station we were pushed into a cell, where we took a nap to recuperate; when we woke we felt aggrieved and hammered on the door till a policeman came. We said it was essential that we see the Commandant, and after a long palaver were hauled before an officer of police. Luckily he was an Englishman, and when we told him we were going to join the Air Force, he relaxed a little. "But," he said, "don't forget to catch that train; I shall have a detective there to see you do." That cell, I reflected, was not a nice cell; it was cold with bare stone, and there were no mattresses. Far better to be a spy than a common disturber of the peace, for they feel that you are a person of consequence and so treat you with respect. We puffed on our pipes thoughtfully for a while, then G.S. asked: "Look, which of us *is* the spy?" "I don't know," I replied. "Are you?" I knew I wasn't, though afterwards I have thought that I missed a great opportunity. Whether G.S. was I neither know nor care, for a man with his outlook would certainly be on the right side.

In the morning we were met by friendly smiles. The films had been developed and there was only one photograph of the aerodrome, almost hidden by Pilkis and myself. But as a gesture they had cut it out, and they returned the rest of the film to G.S. together with a new one. Then they offered to take us back in the car.

The Scandinavian police had sometimes inconvenienced us, but I doubt whether any other police, except perhaps the British, so well combined thoroughness with friendliness and fairness.

About noon we rode down the road that already we had travelled twice by car, till it joined the main road that connects north and south Norway. At the junction stood a signpost stating on one arm "Mosjöen 56," on the other "Trondheim 365." Though Trondheim was still as far away as York from London, we felt we had now come near to it by its very mention upon a signpost, and rode much heartened upon our way southward up the long and straight Svenningelv. Steeply below us to the right the river dropped down in steps, each a powerful waterfall. Here for the first time was traffic, perhaps a couple of dozen cars or lorries in a day, where before three or four had been a busy day, and here there was no forest to side-step into. The road was un-walled and often upon the very edge, which went straight down sometimes three hundred feet to the river. We must pass on the outside, for where in Sweden the rule is keep to the left, in Norway it is to the right. Pilkis must learn better manners. It was not vice, but fear; assurance, not force, was needed. So on the approach of traffic from behind I halted her and turned her to face it, stroking her neck and talking to her quietly to calm her fear. It took a couple of weeks, much patience, and a few unpleasant moments to teach her toler-ance of this rush of traffic.

Here, too, the horses had their first experience of a steam train. We had been welcomed to his red house by a railway-man in charge of a desolate stretch of line. Pilkis had been put in a little stable, while Musti was tied up in a lean-to. As we were feeding them, a freight train rattled round a bend, greeting the railwayman with blasts upon the whistle. Pilkis goggled through the stable window at the monster, too amazed to move; Musti leapt back, breaking his halter, and tore off alongside the train, and went out of sight with it among the trees in what seemed to be a mixture of panic and curiosity. We found him half a mile away with his head down to a patch of grass, the train forgotten.

The Svenningelv, which had flowed against us, at last

dwindled to a slow and stoneless brook straying upon flat brown marsh. As we rode down the other side of the watershed into the Namdal we were joined by another sluggish stream collecting from the marsh, growing at first into a lively beck and then a torrent leaping down on its hundred-mile journey to the sea.

The first night in the Namdal we rode to a little village oddly without a farm. The storekeeper, in the lilting tone of speech of this part of Norway that recalls Welsh or Afrikaans, offered a stable for the horses and the storage loft above the shop for us. We bought food from him and cooked a meal in his paddock in the company of his scheming elk-hound, a breed of dog very common in these parts and one we came to like for his friendliness and intelligence. His origin I do not know, but in appearance he is a cross between a sledge-dog and an Alsatian.

One day at noon we came to a dell of lush grass. Here we unsaddled the horses and chased them to the far end away from the road and lay down in the sun's warmth, for the summer was now opening out. G.S. asked: "D'you know it's Midsummer Day?" I did not, for we had been blessedly unmindful of dates. His thoughts went home. "I should like to be in Copenhagen just for tonight. We make a lot of Midsummer Night all over Scandinavia; I suppose it's because we feel grateful for the summer after the hard winter. In many places they still have bonfires and dance around the maypole. At home we go to our house by the sea; the lawn slopes down to the water's edge and it's lit with Chinese lanterns hung among the trees. We dance and drink and eat with our friends. My father's a born entertainer and great fun. They'll be getting everything ready now." He gazed into the tree-tops in nostalgic silence.

Soon the horses had methodically mown the grass and knowingly stood ready to move on to their next feed. We saddled and went. As we topped a rise there appeared in a homely hollow below us a little red village pierced by its white church steeple, satisfying the thought of night quarters which was growing upon us. We followed our long, beckoning shadows into the village, named Trones on our map.

By the church a man of good, rugged features addressed us shortly. "Are you looking for stables? Put them in there"—and waved towards a large, well-kept building which we had noticed with approval during the descent. We thanked him gratefully and led the horses into the stable. He was of few words. "Hay?" he asked from a mountain of it, piling the racks high. "Oats?"—having poured half a bucketful into each manger. Then he attended to us. "What do you fellows eat? Food?"

G.S., infected by his manner, replied: "Yes, mostly."

"This way."

We followed him into the farm-house.

"Will ham and eggs do?"

They certainly would. In ten minutes, plates covered by hunks of ham and three eggs were put before us. A whole loaf was sliced to pieces; mounds of butter and goat's-milk cheese, cold fish, cream, and jam joined it. A kettle of coffee simmered upon the stove. Our host sat down and joyfully watched us eat; hospitality seen to, he found time for less urgent matters. He presumed we were the fellows who were riding through Norway: how did we like the country? and were we having a good time? and he liked the look of the horses—what breed were they?

That evening brought the most unfortunate setback to the journey so far. On the other side of the Kiolen we had groomed the horses little, taking off only the top dirt to leave the grease in their skins as protection against cold. But now they would be better for a thorough cleaning. We were strapping them in the stable when the farmer, Herr Molberg, came in with a serious expression. He spoke to G.S. "There's just been an S.O.S. on the wireless for you. Your father has had a bad riding-accident and you are wanted at home. They have been trying to get in touch with you for two days."

It was ill news for G.S., though he said nothing to show it. We stopped grooming and went inside. I told him I knew someone who had been unconscious with concussion for three weeks, and still came round afterwards (I didn't, but vaguely remembered hearing of someone who had). We sat silent for a few minutes, staring at the stove, both knowing this meant his return to Copenhagen. I remembered with a sudden shock how he had spoken almost wistfully of the happy time his family would be having tonight. He would be thinking of that now. Then we planned for the inevitable. At Herr Molberg's suggestion, Musti would be left here on the farm. If G.S. was able to come back, he would bring

Musti by train to catch up with me; if not, Herr Molberg would sell him for him. He would take G.S. in his old car to the nearest station to catch the night train for Trondheim and so to Oslo, whence he could fly to Copenhagen. It was all sudden and hard to realize. But neither of us considered for a moment that the ride should be abandoned; it must be completed if with only half our forces. This had long been an understanding with us; on the ship to the North we had agreed that if anything should happen to one of us, the other should proceed alone. Even so early the journey was more than an ambition. If I abandoned it now (and I had no wish to do so), I should be letting down G.S. as much as myself.

We put it into words. G.S. asked: "I suppose you will continue, whether I can get back or not?" I said that I certainly would, and he replied: "That's good; I should like you to." He must have felt far worse than I did, for he was worried about his father and he might be seeing the last of his horse and the journey, and both meant a lot to him. It was an unhappy parting, though nothing was said but the ordinary. We shook hands, he slammed the door, and the car drove into the night, leaving only a bobbing point of redness that died away in the darkness.

At the Molbergs' invitation I stayed the next day on the farm, for Musti was to be put with their two *fjordings*[1] that were roaming in the forest, where now there was plentiful grass in the glades. In the morning I put Pilkis on a patch of

[1] Native Norwegian ponies.

grass by the stable, tethering her by a Norwegian hobble, which fastens round the pastern of one fore-leg. Then we went with Musti. We crossed a broad but not deep river, Herr Molberg crossing unconcernedly to his waist, in shirt and trousers, while I rode Musti through to his belly with my legs tucked up round his neck, for I had no change of trousers.

On the way back from the forest we came upon a party of lumberjacks rolling logs from stacks into the river, to float them down to a sawmill. Now and then one of the logs jammed against a rock, gathering others as they drifted down and piling them up in disorder. Then a couple of men with poles waded out and climbed upon the mass to free it, a job needing skill and a steady head. They had to find the key log, roll off those upon it, and loosen it. Then the mass moved. They jumped from one log to another back towards the bank, sure-footed as they must be, for a slip between logs weighing perhaps a ton could mean being unpleasantly crushed. Musti joined the *fjordings,* but that evening he appeared again before the stables calling to Pilkis, and we had to take him back once more. It seemed that he preferred his old travelling-companion to his new ones.

I made a parcel of my Arctic jacket to send home, for the cold seemed finally left behind and the jacket had become an impediment hanging most of the time across the saddle pommel. Pullovers and thick underclothes had been discarded by the way, for purposely they had been brought from the rag-bag.

The little daughter of the house—six or seven, I should say —was as friendly as her parents. My scanty Norwegian was a handicap to our *affaire*, but she showed her friendliness by frequent offerings of sweets graced by a little curtsy and a sunny-eyed smile on her clear but freckled face.

15. A Man and a Horse

Whose only fit companion is his horse. COWPER

AS Pilkis and I left Trones, a long farewell followed us a mile down the straightness of the road. Each time I turned, two arms waved strongly from the gate of the farm; between them a small bare arm fluttered in child-like abandon.

It was an uneventful day, so that towards its end it was good to see the spray-cloud poised over the great Fiskumfoss (and later the falls' boiling green wall, which halted me in wonderment), for I planned to stay at the Fiskum *gestiveri* a couple of miles further on.

Most of the following day we passed through as beautiful a valley as I have seen, its steep sides coloured with pines, split here and there by thin, far-dropping waterfalls that fed the river resting after the battering of the Fiskumfoss and now drifting green and clear.

The next three days were to pass for the most part in quiet reflection, in approaching and going beside the great Snasavatn, a forty-mile-long lake framed by tree-clad hills and marked here and there by shapely islands. Twice we slept on friendly farms (we were not to come again to the primitive but hospitable *bruk* before the remote *fjells* of the Dovre), and once in a glade beside a track, where curious cattle roused a willing horse and an unwilling man in the early dawn. Later that day upon a hillside I did duty as midwife to a cow having trouble with her stubborn and reluctant calf. In this part of the country and at this time of year both cattle and horses are turned loose in the forests to wander where they will in search of grass, so that often we rode past scattered cattle, or a couple of fat and jaunty *fjordings* with their intelligent Arabian-like heads and clipped and bristly manes would prance up to us to see what sort of horse-and-man this was. It was idyllic, Forest-of-Arden country, its content broken, only slightly, by one event.

I had heard along the road that an Englishman called Mr. Smith was living in the neighbourhood. I thought that if I came to his house I would halt there and hear a little of my own tongue for a change, and perhaps, he, too, might welcome a few minutes' talk with one of his countrymen, for he certainly would not meet many here. As we topped a rise in the road I saw a Union Jack flying from a private house. Now, it may be that the sight of that flag set me off on the wrong foot. Both G.S. and I had brought with us our national flags to pin on the saddle blankets, but we had displayed them less and less frequently. We felt that national pride is an excellent thing, but other people have it, too, and to flaunt one's flag in another and friendly country seems to shout: "Look, I'm British [or whatever it is]; I'm something special." No doubt the best way is to show your own and that of your hosts side by side: to show only your own can be taken for ill-mannered advertisement; to show both equally is friendship, and thus honours your flag. So mine stayed crumpled in my pocket unless I rode by myself; then it was brought out occasionally and with misgivings when I tired of meditation and sought encounter by the wayside, for its one excuse was that it might bring introduction.

I knocked upon the door. A man answered it, and I wished him good-morning and asked if he were Mr. Smith. "No, Major Smith," he answered stiffly. I apologized for my ignorance and we exchanged platitudes for a while. As I went, his wife came out and patted Pilkis and wished me luck upon the way.

Towards the end of the Snasavatn we came to a homely village gathered about the road on the gentle slope from hills to lake. I went to the first farm. A pug-faced, thick-set woman came to the door. I asked her if she had a stall that I might put my horse in for the night. She gave me the biggest surprise of the journey. She exploded at me, as though I were a boy who had thrown a stone through her window or a firework under the door. Her flailing arms showed me the way back to the road, and, too amazed for speech, I went. Riding along the road, I tried to find a reason for this rebuff. I believed that my Norwegian had improved a little; I believed that my request could not have been taken as an insult; I hoped that the words had no other meaning. Half a mile along the road we came to a friendly farm.

Next morning we started early. A low mist, a long gossamer banner, shimmered along the lake in a bright morning sun, promising a warm day. It was such a morning as filled one with unreasoning happiness and so with energy. Pilkis did not seem inclined to trot; knowing her as a willing horse, I took it for tiredness, for yesterday had been long; so I dismounted, both to rest her and to work off my energy. As we went, a blob of froth blew from her mouth upon my sleeve, half-noticed—then another—and another, at last waking my perception that had been dulled by the senses. She was not frothing against her bit in anxiety to be away, but plodding dispassionately by my side. Then why the froth? I stopped and looked at her. She seemed troubled. (A horse is as expressive as a human being, showing in eyes and ears instead of eyes and mouth.) She jerked her head into her breast in a convulsive retch, tensing her curving neck muscles and bringing up a fore-leg as though to ease pain. We stayed still while I watched. Another convulsion, and more froth. Her eyes said plainly: "I don't understand this pain. I am ill, very ill."

Of course she was ill. You damned unthinking fool not to have seen it before! I must undo her girth and take the saddle off. Thank God, there's a farm just up the slope. We'll go there and ring up the vet.

We went slowly, pausing when she brought her head painfully in to her breast. At last we stopped by the door, and the farmer came out. I said: "Will you please ring the nearest vet? My horse is sick; I think it's colic. It's very bad." At once he went to the phone. He was all right—I knew by the concern in his face and his unquestioning action.

I walked her round in slow circles, halting when she retched. It was puzzling. It was like colic, but not the same. At last the vet came and confirmed my rising fear. "She is poisoned; probably she has picked up a poisonous weed"— and answer my blunt, sickened question: "No, I'm afraid there is little hope. But if she is alive by five this afternoon, she will have a chance." He slid a rubber tube down her rigid gullet and poured down a purgative to her stomach.

I led her into the stable and piled her stall with straw. The farmer said sympathetically: "Take as much as you want, I've got plenty [he had very little], and I'll be in the house if I can help." I sat on a milking-stool behind her and waited. Then I walked up and down for a while, and sat down again. I went into her stall and talked to her, and came out feeling that she might be better left alone. The hours were interminable as the convulsions worsened. I kept looking at my watch. Two o'clock. Twenty past. Half past. Quarter to three. It couldn't be long now. Could I make it less painful? No, afraid not—only straw to soften the fall. Twenty past three. The farmer came in to see how she was, and we talked for a while. Four o'clock. I hadn't seen her retch for a bit. She retched again. Optimistic fool. She should have fallen by now. I found myself praying. Anything in the world that might help was worth trying. I stood and watched. . . . Her head hung steady. . . . Still steady. I looked again at my watch. Ten to five. She was better than in the morning. I did not dare to rejoice, but felt a sudden hope. If only six o'clock would come so I could see how she was then . . .

At last she raised her head and looked around, interested. Yes, interested. The pain was gone from her eyes. I went into her stall, deeply thankful, and stroked her neck and nose. There was no doubt now. She was past the worst.

Each hour till midnight I fed her a handful of hay, no more than a rabbit would eat, and then lay down upon a heap of straw in front of her stall and slept fitfully, while from time to time she woke me with a soft soliciting nose for yet another mouthful of hay. It was the happiest night of many upon our long journey.

We stayed for a couple of days on this friendly farm, Pilkis resting and increasing her rations and strength, myself writing long-delayed letters and eating bacon and eggs ("The English always eat bacon and eggs," the kind farm-wife told me), and I did my best to thank them for their kindness. The farmer and I spent many hours increasing our scanty knowledge of each other's language, and I hope that it repaid him a little for his kindness. As was our habit, I asked if I might pay for Pilkis's hay, to give an opportunity to pay for my own food as well if he accepted and avoid offending him if he would not. As I expected from his open-handedness, he would not take a penny. "No," he said simply; "it was good to help you and your horse when she was ill."

We left in the afternoon on a short stage of some six miles to Steinkjer. I rested Pilkis much, so that as we came slowly into the town a public clock showed after ten. This was the first town (though a small one) that we had come to in Norway. It had been bombed flat by the Luftwaffe during the war, and its hygienic modernity was too respectable to contain farm stables, making it a poor place for a Polar rider. For the first time I missed the delightful Scandinavian way of bringing their compact farms into the villages, just as they sailed their ships between their houses.

I asked a night-stroller where I might find a stable. "The only stables here are down by the quay; you'll be able to get in and there'll be hay there," he said. They were very large and roomy, and I presumed they must belong to a market. There was hay and plenty of straw; I gathered armfuls of both, filled a rack with hay, and laid down a bed deep enough to please a hunter. Pilkis seemed very content.

It was late now, so I heaped straw in the adjoining stall for my bedding and made a resolution for a good breakfast in the morning. Before turning in, I was called out by the smell of salt to watch the evening leisure of fat fishing-boats at rest against the quay.

In the morning I woke to find an unpleasant-looking fellow hovering at the bottom of my stall. He was drunk and spoke thickly. It was obvious that he was not the owner of the stables and also that he was out to be awkward. I answered his jabbering in English, playing for time while I pulled on my boots. He waved towards Pilkis, telling me to take her out. Now booted and standing, I explained in Norwegian our predicament, that we had come in late last night and could find nowhere else, and that I would of course pay for the stabling and fodder but should like to give her something to eat before we went. He waved drunkenly again and lurched towards her to untie her halter rope. I moved in on her other side and got to her rope first. He put out his hand to it, at the same time knocking her across in the stall roughly. In a sudden rage at this rough handling, I knocked his hand down and rapped out: "Keep your hands off her, you bastard." He cursed and put out his hand again, and I drew back my fist to smack it in his bleary face. He saw it through his drunkenness and his instinct told him that a slow-moving drunken man, even with the advantage of weight, was likely to have the worst of it with a sober man in a mood ripe for murder. He dropped his hand and went gibbering away. Soon he was back with another man, who wanted to know what I was doing here. I explained, and his face lit with understanding. "Oh, you're the Englishman who has ridden from the North? I saw it in the paper"—and asked if I liked Norway and if I was having a good time, and a dozen more questions. Of course I must give the horse a feed—I must help myself—while the toss-pot stood deflated in the background, obviously an underling.

It was only as we were about to leave that I knew that we had slept in the stables of a slaughterhouse. Scandinavia, as a whole, is advanced in good treatment of animals to be slaughtered, in contrast with the Latin countries and, where horse-slaughtering is concerned, with our own as well. Thus they build the stables away from the slaughterhouses so that animals have no premonition of their fate.

As we went out of Steinkjer a car pulled up before us and a man got out holding a camera. He asked in good English: "I hope you don't mind my taking your photo?" I lied: "No," shortly, but when he began to talk, his friendliness slowly blew away my ill-humour. His wife, it seemed, was English. "I'm sure she'd like to meet you. Have you a few minutes to spare? My place is over there," and he pointed to a notice upon a photographer's studio—"Martin Knoph." I felt that I had been churlish. Also, I had not spoken with an English person (excepting the major) since leaving the ship at Bergen. It is pleasant to meet someone from home when in a foreign country if you don't meet too many and for too long. They were a friendly couple, so when it was suggested I stay the night, I readily agreed—"Providing," I said, "you know a good place where I can put my horse." "Oh yes," he replied, "we have a good farmer friend half a mile up the hill. We'll ring him at once. But there's plenty of grass in the garden; it could do with eating-down. Put her there while you have something to eat."

So in half an hour Pilkis gorged on fresh grass while I gorged on Mrs. Knoph's good food. Fortunately, she was a woman of discernment and looked on a good appetite as a tribute to cooking—at least, I hope so. That night I slept in a soft bed with clean sheets while Pilkis, her belly full of corn, sprawled across a kindly stable. It was one of our good nights.

In the morning I went to the post office to gather letters; there were none, but a cable from G.S. said: "Shall be at Trones on Tuesday. Please ring." Today was Tuesday. When I rang, G.S. answered; it was good to hear him. "I'll bring Musti by train tomorrow. What about meeting at Sparbu? It's about fifteen kilometres beyond Steinkjer. There's a freight train gets in about noon. How are you and that minx Pilkis?" So we talked hurriedly till our time was up and then: "Cheerio; see you tomorrow," and clamped down the phone. His father had recovered consciousness and was mending, so G.S. had taken the plane to Trondheim and trained to Trones. Two hours later Pilkis and I were on the road to Sparbu.

16. We Call on the Devil

When once the trumpet of fame has sounded a poor man's name, farewell to his repose for ever. VOLTAIRE

IN the morning I went to meet the train, to find it already resting at the station. It was very long and assorted, headed by a complicated engine with a brass bell and many wheels and domes. The Norwegian trains recalled those of the American nineties as shown on the films, and the likeness was completed by their habits of burrowing in and out of mountains, traversing crags with the nicest of judgment, and gliding across chasms on flimsy bridges. I imagine there are as many gymnastics to the kilometre for Norwegian trains as any in the world, and the traveller who could find no interest from his window would be blind indeed.

Around a cattle truck was activity which suddenly split in two and piled up to the outside, and a mettled Musti tore out with G.S. on the end of his halter rope. There was recognition and a medley of hand-shaking and slapping and whinneying and gleeful attempts at kicking.

Today was the most talkative of the journey, for there was much to tell of the last ten days and much to decide for the future. G.S. told of his arrival at the Copenhagen airport on a hot summer day and of the astonishment at his fur hat and Arctic jacket; of his finding that his taste for his native Tuborg and Carlsberg was still active; of the announcement, bellowed in his ear at the horse show, of his brother's display of trick riding: "the brother of Gorm Skifter, who is at present riding through the snows of Lapland"; of the flask of whisky, and the choice piece of Old Holsteiner cheese for me (tapping his saddle-bag). I alternated with my progress in his absence and abuse of his new appearance in riding-boots and breeches, till the rugged coastal road by Röra quieted us by its splendour; and when it came to its end, evening had come and we must look for quarters. We found them on a prosperous farm. Here they bred *fjordings*, but these were up in the *fjells* for the summer and the roomy stables offered our horses choice of stalls.

This was the beginning of the richest farming-country I was to see on the whole journey, one of the few moderately flat parts of Norway. Well-kept red or yellow farm-houses and stables studded the vivid green fields of sown grass and clover. Here would be no vain searches for food and shelter; plenty surrounded us, and press publicity had carpeted the way. People saw us from afar and came offering breakfast, lunch, tea, dinner, and infinite coffee, and the horses a harvest of hay and oats. It was almost embarrassing and, as we knew, undeserved, but people were so friendly and insistent that to refuse more than was needful for progress would be churlish. Here for the first time we faced food without hunger and so enjoyed it the less.

Sometimes our hosts asked us to write or draw something as a memento. The Dane usually drew an amusing caricature of the Lapland journey showing a horse grinning at a bandy Lapp before his tent. When I suggested that the Lapp had the better reason for grinning and the horse for being bandy, he assured me that this was Art seen through the eyes of the horse and that all human beings look ridiculous to other creatures. I said no more, for I felt he had something there. My offering was always the same: a side view of a mare's head and neck with a deeply curving Arab profile and a naughty and flirtatious eye. (Always the same because this is the only drawing I can do, apart from one of an elephant seen from behind, used to illustrate a slightly bawdy tale.)

Always on a long journey you come without warning to a place instantly liked. So it was with Levanger, a little town with wooden buildings standing on stilts from the fiord. We rode the horses to their bellies into the water, where they pawed joyfully to drench their flanks and our boots, for all day they had gone in the dust of coastal tracks dried by the almost circling summer sun. Here Nature was sucked up from its still-damp roots and shot up in its heyday; but soon the sun would drop and the cold rain would come to warn of the advancing snow perhaps already probing the northern coast of Lapland.

Next day we rode by the Aasen fiord, where the *Tirpitz*

hid till it was found and bombed and scurried to yet another hiding-place. An old farmer told us sadly that his windows had been smashed, which he did not mind; but the *Tirpitz* had not been, which he did mind.

We left Aasen by a track over a low hill; from the top was a far-going view down the Trondheim fiord, a harmony of blues and greens reaching almost to the open sea, speckled here and there upon its southern shores by the white houses of little villages. We sat there peacefully for a while and then went down to Hell.

It was a pleasant little place, clustering in the manner of an English village rather than in the widespread Norwegian fashion. It is the Right Thing for British and American visitors to laugh long in Hell; the locals listen indulgently to the perennial puns, then offer for expensive sale a stamp picturing the devil himself, tailed, horned, and happily burning. The inhabitants smile, the foreigners laugh, the devil leers, and so everyone is pleased.

As G.S. was riding along the street a hundred yards in front of me, I saw a woman step out and speak to him for a moment. As I came level she stepped out again with her hand outstretched. "Will you take this krone? It might buy something." A krone is worth a shilling, and, even allowing for our appearance of beggars on horseback (or perhaps because of it?), this was an embarrassing offer. My instinct was to refuse it, but her motive seemed to be genuine. So, wishing I might disappear into the saddle-wallets, I took the krone and thanked her as though she offered a five-pound note.

When I caught up with G.S. he told me he had refused his krone; which was the better thing to do we did not know, but we both wished she had not offered those kroner.

The owner of the café came out and invited us to coffee and cakes. We tried to refuse, but persistence seemed to mean offence, as though we scorned her kindliness, so we went in to drink the excellent coffee and cream and eat rich cake while the two waitresses hovered whispering around the serving door, perhaps surprised that we ate almost normally. Ungraciously we thought how welcome such an interlude as this would have been so many times in the past.

A farm track brought us to Hommelvik, a growing little town with a flying-boat anchorage and light industry. It spread round a broad bay that led up to a stubby valley; from the higher ground behind, a tower dominated the town like a judge his court. This, we were told, was part of a big farm, the buildings of which could be seen grouped around the tower.

When we came to the farm, the prosperity imagined from afar proved to be an illusion. The clock in the tower was still, its face tired and grey; the once-red buildings a streaked and washed-out pink, like the bottom of a ship long due for paint. Grass grew long among the rusting wreckage of a mower. Only before the house was there cut grass and a neat bed of flowers. Here we knocked and were welcomed. We were shown the horse stable, and its mangers were heaped with fresh-cut grass.

Above the many stables and store-rooms branched empty

barns at right angles one from the other, cavernous and hollow. Heavy floors sagged, and sprung and creaked to the tread; here and there was a dark gap where a plank had fallen into the darkness below. In corners and crevices cobwebs had laced together clusters of musty seeds from hay used long ago. Everywhere was the sad desolation of an emptiness where once had massed gatherings of the harvest to feed the animals that sheltered below from the winter. Time's decay could not wait for a clock. In such a place a man might be forgiven for seeing a ghost on a winter's night, with the wind whining through gaps between the planks of the walls, the creaking and shifting of old giant timbers, and distorted shadows from the intricate pattern of beams falling across a wrinkled floor.

We were invited to breakfast, and an excellent one it was, too. They were gracious people, and the house was well and tastefully furnished. It seemed that the farm had fallen into disrepair during the German occupation; now there was only one son left at home to work it, and the task of repairing the vast stables was too great.

Word of the strange travellers' arrival had gone round Hommelvik. What seemed to be the entire population had turned out in the main street. Now we were to be embarrassed not only by too much hospitality, but by sight-seeing also. You have to have done a very big thing to be able to go down a lane of waving, well-wishing people without feeling a fool and a cheat. We did not blame these people, whose friendliness we knew well, but we deplored the disproportionate publicity created by the press seeking sensation. We doubted how to receive this welcome; to wave to right and left and switch on a faceful of teeth like a film star or a boxer was pantomime, and fatuous; to ride unsmilingly ahead was unfriendly, and this was even worse. Behaviour abroad is important, for there you represent not only yourself, but your countrymen. What did happen was that we chatted to each other as though there was no one else within miles or smirked like schoolboys coming on to sing at a school concert. In either case we no doubt looked unutterably silly. The only times we felt normal and at ease were when one or two pretty girls blew us kisses. To that we responded as any man would.

The coastal road to Trondheim was brilliant in the sun, its summer bungalows scoured white, as though fresh from a blueing in the Mediterranean-like sea. Life was luxurious, and this as a change was delightful. We pulled off our shirts and vests and draped them over the saddle pommels, offering our backs to the benevolent sun.

Slow, unconscious riding is music. The slight sway in time with the movement of your horse and the regular beat of hoofs are as satisfying and rhythmic as a tango, yet effortless as the swinging of your arms when you walk and soothing as a rocking-chair. We felt no envy of the people who waved to us from motor cars, and some of those who stopped to ask if they might take a photograph or to offer us a cigarette or just to be friendly followed their farewell waves by wistful backward looks through the window as if wondering, perhaps for the first time, whether a car's soft seat in some way caused them to miss the spice of travelling.

In the early afternoon we saw below us by the sea a range of stables in the shape of a cross and large enough to hold the horses of a regiment. There were still five miles to Trondheim; we did not know how we should fare there for stables, as farms could hardly be expected in the town. It seemed better to put up the horses here if we could, rather than go in possibly futile search around Trondheim. Our usual undeserved good fortune was with us: we were shown into stables as fine as I have seen anywhere. At one time they had been used for race-horses; now they were empty but provided with food and bedding, for the larger part of the building was a cow barn. We inquired about a magnificent stone building near by, reminiscent of an early Victorian mansion: it seemed it was an asylum. The harmless cases were allowed to wander about the grounds: two or three came and spoke to us, and one said how lucky we were that they let us bring our horses with us. These were about the only people we met who regarded us as in no way unusual, which was perhaps a little ominous.

17. Return to Trondheim

Après bon vin bon cheval. FRENCH PROVERB

IT was good to see the horses resting in well-earned luxury. We strapped and groomed them as for a show, combing and brushing manes and tails so often matted and caked with dirt; their clean sawdust bedding was smoothed and their racks stuffed with hay. It was tempting to heap their mangers with oats, but we restrained ourselves from this cruel kindness; we might give ourselves colic in our rare orgies, but it was done with open eyes and there would be no lasting harm. "Pity," we said, "we can't take them to the best hotel in Trondheim, fill 'em solid with lobster and caviar and good wine, and put them in the best suite, as they deserve." Yet when their feed was finished, they stood awkwardly in their roomy boxes as though embarrassed by these aristocratic quarters, as a labourer might be in Buckingham Palace. They felt perhaps a lack of homeliness in this expensive spaciousness. It was misplaced modesty; they had done a job too tough for any thoroughbred and come in winners.

A distant whistle of a train reminded us to go into Trondheim; hastily we patted the polished rumps, slammed the stable doors, and on legs stiff from long riding set out like startled turkeys across country and over the railway fencing, pulling ourselves onto the platform before an indignant train. As G.S. said, we'd spent three months coming for this train and nearly missed it in the end.

On our journey north by ship, Trondheim had seemed what it is, a town of less than sixty thousand inhabitants. Now it seemed to have spread out in our absence, its approaches by train as processional as those of Euston and its buildings grown higher. So much are impressions measured relatively and by the immediate rather than the more remote past; to us a *bruk* had taken on the importance of a village, and a village a city.

I have no description of Trondheim to offer, for this has been done by better pens than mine. And, what is more important, I know little of the town, for our spare moments were taken up without profit but with pleasure by the fascination of the comings and goings in the harbour. But we saw enough to know it as a tranquil town.

There was much to be done. Firstly there was celebration. Trondheim had long been a milestone in the journey; it marked the end of the middle and the beginning of the south; here we might at last look back upon the route marked on the map and say: "Well, we've come a good way and now we're on the home straight"—which would be an excellent opportunity of feeling pleased with ourselves, and that, of course, is paradise. The new comfort of summer clothes, and much-needed camera film, awaited us; there was mail at the post office; and in Trondheim there are many baths. Here, too, I would have a much-needed haircut, but G.S. scorned this yielding to convention and stated his determination to go uncut to Denmark. By now his fair, curling beard and hair were boldly leonine, so that he needed only a horned helmet to look like a noble Dane of old.

We went first to the British Consulate, for it was by the station. The Consul was standing at the far end of his office, looking from the window. He turned at the opening of the door and stared for a moment before he exclaimed: "Good God, where have you fellows come from? We thought you'd got lost in a snowdrift in Finnmark"—and came to us with a smile and gave us a welcoming hand. He asked much about the journey and then chaffed us about our beards, putting us at a disadvantage in reply, for they were poor rough shags beside his silky, well-kept beard.

Neither of us cares to do things by halves; neat, or not at all. We had determined to relax in Trondheim, so we must relax to the utmost, in luxury. We should stay at the best hotel and eat the best food—and that, we were told, meant the Britannia. Field-Marshal Montgomery had stayed there two days before and had been enthusiastically welcomed; I hoped this next Englishman would not let his country down too badly by comparison. But I fear he did.

The reception desk received our barbarity coldly; the hall porter disapproved of our travel-stained and outlandish persons, regarding us from seared boots and well-worn breeches to patched shirts and weather-scarred faces. With simultaneous puckish impulse we draped our saddle-wallets upon his shrinking arms and made known a wish to be shown to our rooms. We followed his embarrassed dignity past well-dressed guests.

Dinner was already being served, so after a vigorous scouring we went down to the dining-room. Its centre was sunken and ornately paved, and there fountains played into a pond. It was all very, very luxurious. The diners regarded us with surprise, the surprise that would meet a man in tails going into a transport café—that of incongruity.

But the food was excellent. Lustily we ate hors d'œuvres, revelled in lobster with wine sauce, sturdily attacked large underdone steaks. We dallied over peach melba and coffee. And from time to time sipped a bottle of good French wine, for this was an Occasion and worthy to be savoured.

Relaxation such as this must lead to reminiscence and happy thoughts of the future. So we talked quietly and contentedly till early morning, when yawns interrupted and we became aware that we were now alone in the spacious lounge. We rose and stretched ourselves and let the lift take us up to bed.

The shoes put on the horses at Hattfjelldal had been of poor, soft stuff compared with the first shoeing with Kiruna metal, and at the toes were now worn down almost to the hoof. We cast round for advice about a blacksmith. The one at the trotting-track was good, we were told. We ran him to earth, took the horses to the track smithy, and had them shod, all in a couple of hours, and rode back to the stables feeling new and satisfactorily equipped to face life. The horses, too, seemed to take a pride in their new state and stepped out the better for it.

These two days in Trondheim were proving hard on our pockets. The last thing we wished to do was to commercialize the journey, but we could not risk cutting it short by lack of money. We discussed how we might make a little. The plan that might bring in the best return in the shortest time with the least effort (that is, of course, the ideal method) seemed to be offered by the press. True, they had eased our coming where otherwise there might have been doubts of our respectability, yet this had been incidental, a by-product of their scoop. Towards Swedes and Norwegians we shall always feel friendliness and gratitude whenever we think of this journey, but reporters, like waiters, are international and a type of their own. There had been one or two pleasant exceptions, but while the world demands a sensational press there will always be unscrupulous and arrogant reporters. We had no qualms about exploiting them if we could. At the same time, we felt we should like entertainment. To canvass each newspaper office might keep us from poverty but was unlikely to provide much entertainment. So we decided to hold an auction in the hotel; this would at least be amusing and, as far as we knew, original.

G.S. phoned newspaper offices: "Hello? I'm one of the fellows who are riding from Lapland. I wonder if you're interested in the story." Yes, they all were, and their reporters would meet us in the Britannia. "Yes, at two o'clock."

Now, the hall of the Britannia is dominated by an impressive table, very long and very heavy, of the type the films show for meetings of big business. At each end reign high-backed chairs, along one side is an interminably long sofa. At five to two, G.S. and I occupied these chairs; at two minutes to, the first reporter invaded with camera-man. They were most pleased to meet us. They knew, of course, of our extraordinary journey, and thought us wonderful. We smirked modestly. It was a jolly little party. At two the second pair came: we gave introductions and there was a stiff bowing and reserved hand-shaking. The first arrivals seemed less pleased to meet us.

The third and fourth contingents arrived: more introductions, more stiff touching of hands—"Please, gentlemen, be seated"—magnanimous hands indicating the sofa. They sat. Graciously we offered cigarettes.

I began: "Well gentlemen, we believe your papers are interested in this ride. We should, of course, love to give you all the information you wish, but we are poor men as you can see"—with a sad and apologetic gesture towards my shirt and breeches—"and we must live" (like Voltaire, they did not seem to see the necessity). "Now what are you prepared to pay for the copyright story?" And G.S. jumped in. "Yes, we will sell it to the highest bidder. Now, what will you offer?"—raising his fist like an auctioneer's hammer to knock down to the buyer. Confusion. Indecision. Crisis brought them to their feet and knitted them together secretly, old rivals joined together by a common enemy. G.S. and I stood deserted, faces expressionless but eyes exchanging the laughter inside us. Then the huddle straightened and erupted through the door, casting off one for a moment to inform us, icily, that they would see their editors. The tables and the chairs again took on their silent authority. Dignity had come back to the Britannia's hall.

Next morning we hurried to buy papers. The first one we opened, under a heading, *The Riding Beards come to Trondheim,* said shortly:

Yesterday the two dishevelled riders arrived in Trondheim. In the Britannia Hotel they attempted to dictate terms to the press but found it was not to be trifled with. We cannot see why these two have aroused so much interest by their stunt. There is of course nothing new in this ride; horses have been used for travel for a thousand years.

We left Trondheim by the Kongsvei, the old historic road that is a relic of the days when Trondheim was the royal city and is now almost forgotten and unused by all but the country people. For two days we followed its windings among hills now green and gentle in the summer sun. There were occasional signs of industry: the chimney of a brick-works; the whirring of sawmills; the weaving of trains, black-headed snakes, along the sweeping line. But more frequently there were farms, and often people came out to talk to us. One kindly old woman, white-haired and wrinkled and bent upon her sticks, was leading her fat horse in a stubby cart; she stopped and spoke with us, discussing the horses capably and asking of our travels before hobbling on her steadfast way.

On the third day it was good to see the *fjells* heightening and closing in: this was more the Norway that had grown upon us. At Stören that evening we heard that everyone had gone to a wedding at a near-by farm, and G.S. had a bright idea. We would go to that farm and see the celebrations, which we hoped would be held in traditional style. At these country weddings travellers are a good omen and doubly welcome.

So it was that guests, gathered at dusk in groups around the old homestead, saw a strange visitation coming up the winding track towards them—two ragged, bearded men on horseback. The bride's mother came out and welcomed us to the wedding feast; we must come in and eat, we must stable the horses, we must stay the night. We took fish soup and platefuls of meat and drank beer and talked with friends and relations.

Disappointingly, there was no traditional costume, but there was the fiddler who strolled with his playing from group to group, and the uninvited distant relations who came in fancy dress and with masked or blackened faces and were allowed to stay if no one could guess their identity. And of course no one did. Then there was more food and more beer and more fiddling, and the bride and the bridegroom and their parents made speeches of tactful brevity.

In the morning the bride's mother thanked us for coming, and we thanked her for hospitality and went on our way again, into the steepening *fjells*. To the west were the twisted Trollheimen, the trolls' home; to the east the drooping tail of the Kiolen; to the south and before us, the Dovrefjell and the Gudbrandsdal, country of tradition and folklore, of the sagas and Peer Gynt. Dwellings became more scattered and more crabbed; less painted, less horizontal, less perpendicular. And over all, Mount Dovre reigned beneath its snows— Dovre, which is the physical sign of Norwegian patriotism, upon which the National Assembly in 1814 swore:

> *To be faithful and true, one to all*
> *Throughout all time, till Dovre fall.*

And when you see Dovre's mass, you know it for a dreadful oath.

18. Journey in the Past

The older the fiddle, the sweeter the tune. PROVERB

THE high moorland of the Dovre is perhaps as blessedly behind the times as any part of Norway but the Setesdal. It is a Rip Van Winkle of a country, awakening only on its fringes at Opdal and Dombas, and though it has neither the beauty of the fiords nor the grandeur of the Jotunheimen, it has more tradition. And, alluring to a horseman, it is laced with old, overgrown roads and bridle-paths. Near Opdal we came out on one of these paths, its stones now overgrown by reasserting grass and weeds.

Today was washing-day. A shirt dangling from one saddle and a vest from the other added to the accoutrements of wallets and groundsheets, so that only a couple of frying-pans were needed to complete our resemblance to the White Knight. We rode in quiet relaxation, reins dangling loose upon the horses' necks, puffs of smoke rising blue and slow from our pipes against the sunny green of the trees and mingling with the balm of pines and sweating horse in what is for me the most fragrant of all scents, its quality perhaps nostalgic rather than intrinsic.

Soon the track had climbed through the trees and come out upon the open *fjell* side. Down on the left the wooded valley jealously confined the modern tentacle between its pines, but the old track rolled over the *fjells* in the freedom of the up-land air and spacious views. The short and springy turf that often grows upon disused ways gave kindly beneath the horses' hoofs, good both to their tendons and their riders' seats. So time passed pleasantly, till towards evening we came to an old farm straddling the track. It was dark and heavy with old timber, great trunks rough-hewn and weather-beaten. Barns overhung by cocklofts stood up on rock stilts (*stabur,* as they are known) beyond the reach of snow and rats. Grass growing in half a foot of soil fantastically covered the roofs as a barrier against cold and completed the build-ings' harmony with the earth.

Here in the Dovre men had felled great trees thick as the barrel of a horse, hacked off their bark, and heaved and levered them untrimmed one upon the other to make the walls of their barns and houses, the wooden counterparts in age and sturdiness of the Elizabethan manor-house. We had come into Norway's wild old heart, a land of giants and trolls and hobgoblins.

The farm-wife and her three sons made us welcome. We must come inside and eat. But, hungry as we were, our eyes feasted first. The great kitchen had come from the forest:

walls and floor and ceiling were of planks cut from giant tree-trunks. Cupboards painted blue and ornamented in reds and yellows stood in corners; upon a long and lusty sideboard were hand-carved wooden eating- and drinking-bowls, each an individual in the beauty of its graining and the mellow polish that no process but time and use can give. The fireplace, that reached from floor to ceiling, was cylindrical and of hewn stone, displaying in the cavern of its mouth a spit and massive wrought hooks. Now in the summer it gaped clean and cool, waiting for the winter's logs when again the storm-blown snow would come down from the *fjells* to howl around the house like a hungry wolf.

One of the sons, seeing our interest in craftsmanship, brought in an old saddle. It was not like any we had ever seen, but resembled the upper half of a round-backed office chair, mounted on a saddle-tree and panels to fit a horse's back, and covered with time-worn but still rich-red velvet embroidered with gold thread and dated 1793. Its rider sat sideways with her feet upon a rest (for it was a bridal saddle that had taken the family brides to church for a century and more). This saddle must have added to many a touch of pageantry—and not so long ago, for the last to go to church upon it was our hostess. There seemed to be one discord—a photograph upon the wall of a line of dejected men in uniform faced by one in civilian clothes and wearing a belt with a huge revolver. It was a poor photograph both in design and technique. Later the farm-wife explained it to us proudly: this was her husband, who had been a leader of the Resist-

ance during the war, receiving surrender from the Nazis at
its end. Now that we knew the subject, it was no longer discordant.

Next morning we saw a farmer on a horse coming down
from a farm and turning onto the track before us. "D'you
know," said G.S., "that he's the only rider we've seen?" He
was right. Horses pulling carts there had been from time to
time since we came into Norway, but this was the first horse
and rider. We had a fellow feeling for them, such as an Englishman in the middle of the Sahara would feel if he came
across an Arab with a cricket bat. As he came up he nodded
to us. "Nice day for a ride," he said placidly and ambled past,
his far-seeing country-man's eyes upon the distant *fjells*. That
he did not stop was disappointing, for we should have liked
to discuss our mutual interest.

For the next two days we went through a land of becks
and waterfalls, so that it seemed we were always riding into
or coming out of becks. Once or twice we crossed tumbling
rivers by primitive suspension bridges. The first one we came
upon suddenly from a forest track, dangling fifty feet above
a powerful *elv* turgid with melted snow and glacier and
swelling up high above hidden rocks. As we led the horses
onto it, the yard-wide bridge swayed and sprang so that we
crossed one at a time, doubting this simple structure of wood
slung from steel cables. Perhaps its creaks and gratings were a
mere flexing of its joints, but we were glad to reach the other
side.

There were no happier moments on the journey than those

: 183 :

when we pitched camp high in the *fjells* and turned the horses loose to graze, safe now from wolf or bear. The *fjells* rolled away around us as though to the world's end, some smooth and green, others stark and piled with snow, but all friendly and all beautiful. To the southwest the horizon was the Jotunheimen, a far tumult of snow streaked and spotted; to the southeast the jagged Rondane, and to the west the Trollheimen, the "Home of the Trolls." Here and there, where the *fjells* dipped down, lakes had, it seemed, lain among them to sleep. Once or twice an eagle or a kite wound down from the darkening sky, its cry the only competitor of the persistent rumour of a waterfall. We sat against the inside of our saddles, which were stood upon their pommels (few chairs are more satisfactory than those with seats of springy turf and backs and arms of saddle-panels, which fit as well round a man's back as a horse's), and absorbed the calm that settles down upon mountains at the day's end. At last your pipe burns down for the last time and you leisurely spread out your sleeping-bag beside a fire long fallen from its zenith and now glowing red like a settling autumn sun. And the moment you put down your head, you fall asleep in a cool, refreshing night effervescing with stars.

The inner Dovre begins at Drivstua. Here is a mountain hospice in a valley fenced by desolate *fjells*. We spent half a day fishing for trout with borrowed rods while a bitter wind whipped the beck and hunched us shivering into our now light clothes. The catch was one trout by G.S. Henceforth the occasional appearance of *The Compleat Angler* was greeted by him with a raised eyebrow: my angling reputation had suffered a reverse.

The beck was crossed by a kind of self-help cableway, a wooden platform some four feet square slung from pulleys on a steel cable suspended from trestles, one on each bank. You sat upon the platform and hauled yourself with many pulls and much swaying across the fifty yards of beck. It was primitive and efficient.

In the morning we ferried saddlery and equipment by this cableway and swam the horses through the beck. Soon we were riding up a gorge cramped between the *fjells,* beside the Dovre railway, which here hacks its way at three thousand feet along the *fjell* sides, burrowing in and out of them and sometimes disappearing into wooden sheds that protect it from avalanches.

That night I joined the horses in the stable of the Kongsvoll hospice while G.S. slept inside, for a violent bout of rheumatism had gripped his shoulders and his neck had set stiff as a statue's. It was amusing to anyone else to see him half-turn Musti when he wished to see behind him. I massaged his neck and shoulders vigorously with saddle-soap brought back with him from Denmark, while he bore it bravely. But in the morning he was better. Ten days later my left leg set solid at the knee and it was G.S.'s turn for amusement to see me mount from the offside and ride straight-legged as a medieval trooper. Nature was mildly protesting against our liberties.

From Kongsvoll we took a wide and grassy pony track

that crossed at four or five thousand feet over Mount Hjerkinno. The view was expansive, its furthest and highest horizon varied by snow. Below and southward was a table-land
of marsh and forest cracked faintly by the track we were
soon to take. To the west rose tangled Snöhetta, once thought
to be the highest mountain in Norway until the Jotunheimen
were explored at the beginning of last century and later
measured.

The table-land proved to be as dismal as Hjerkinno had
been elevating. The track became straight, flat, and flinty,
sunk between featureless moorland till it came out upon the
Fokstumyr, a lonely marsh that reached out almost to Dombas, a day's journey away. It, too, was flat and without beauty,
but there was a weird desolation reminiscent of the northern
Swedish marshes, and, like them, it was fascinating in its solitude.

Dusk was deepening when we saw in the flat distance a
large white building standing solitary as a ship upon the
ocean. Half a mile from it we came to a track leading directly
to it: a faded signpost said simply: "Winter Way." It was as
tempting as all short cuts, but we avoided it, knowing that
it would be passable only when frozen by the winter. So we
kept to the road till a path led away to the right heralded by
another weather-worn sign: *"Fokstua."* As we rode towards
the building we saw two other smaller ones overshadowed
by it, and that all were in decay became more obvious as we
drew nearer. Tired white paint peeled from the wooden
walls, and blinds hung crookedly in rows of windows. But a

field showed signs of cultivation, and in it two *fjordings* pranced towards us inquisitively. I held the horses while G.S. went to the largest of three entrances and knocked upon the door. An echo reverberated from the interior; it died down, and there was silence once more. Twice more he knocked, and then we went round to the back and searched the windows for human signs. There was nothing but faded blinds and here and there a long-hung lace curtain the colour of newspaper yellowed in the sun. Stone steps led up to a small door; he went up and knocked. It was opened by a woman who regarded us warily; G.S. spoke with her and in a few minutes returned. "It's a queer place this, but she says we can put the horses in the stable and she's asked us to go inside." This barracks seemed a vaster desolation than the miles of empty marsh where it stood alone, perhaps because the marsh was as it was meant to be and had not this unnatural emptiness. She said: "No. 29 will be best" and led us up carpetless stairs to a long and carpetless landing, its undulations giving and creaking to our hollow steps.

As we ate a meal our hostess explained this dilapidation. "People used to come here from Oslo for the ski-ing. Then the Germans came during the war. There were many soldiers and they stayed here a long time. They made us work for them, and they killed most of the animals. They ruined all the furniture and carpets, and now we cannot afford to buy more, so hardly anybody comes. It's all empty now." Her face had turned bitter, but quickly changed to a friendly smile. "You are English and Danish; you are welcome. Please eat more"—and she passed a plate heaped with goat's-cheese sandwiches. Almost everywhere in Norway it was the same: a hatred of German soullessness and a friendliness for the English.

We left early next morning for Dombas by a track that had once been the posting-road. We did not stay there long, for, like Opdal, it is out of harmony with the Dovre. We went from it steeply down to the village of Dovre.

In the morning we crossed a primitive wooden bridge onto a rough farm track climbing gradually along the hillside that soon turned into an ever-steepening valley. The day had turned warm and sunny, and we took off our shirts to feel the coolness of the mountain air. The track came to a cluster of *bruks* marked on the map as Jonndalen. Over cups of coffee we were given directions on crossing the *fjells* to Vagavatn, a long lake that separates Dovre from the Jotunheimen. Leading the horses, we climbed steeply up the side of a *fjell* along a track too narrow for one horse to pass another, coming out upon a ridge that led to the top of the pass. Sheep lay near by in a patch of snow to cool their thickly woolled bodies. At times the track faded among low bushes and twice we had to return to pick it up once more, till at last we saw below us the little village of Vaga by a reach of the lake.

Next day we rode by the lake on the last of the old Dovre tracks, for the next stage would take us into the Jotunheimen, the "Home of the Giants." Outside Lom that night we stayed at a rugged old farm built of the largest whole trunks we ever saw, its small and latticed windows giving it a strangely

Elizabethan aspect. The wooden ceiling, walls, and floor of the great living-room were unpainted, and polished only by time. Gay rugs and tapestries coloured the otherwise sombre tones. We were shown an immense old Bible two feet square and six inches thick, written by hand and bound in brass, matching the bulk of the house. It seemed it was one of the first Norwegian Bibles, written in Danish, which was at that time the official language of Norway.

The stables were of the same massive timbers, with stalls and boxes roomier than most suburban dining-rooms, and a ceiling supported by pillars of tree trunks but low and dark so that it was more like the cellars of an old château than a stable. But it must have been a grand, warm place for a horse in the winter.

At noon next day we stopped in Lom to eat and look at its thirteenth-century wooden stavechurch, which had long since yellowed with age beneath its spires. It was an apt farewell to Dovre.

19. Home of the Giants

The sounding cataract
Haunted me like a passion; the tall rock,
The mountain, and the deep and gloomy wood,
Their colours and their forms, were then to me
An appetite; a feeling and a love.

WORDSWORTH

AFTER Lom came a change in Nature and in history. Behind us was the man-made tradition of the Dovre, its stave-church, its grotesque folk-lore carvings, and the robust maturity of its farms. Before us was the Jotunheimen. There was a sudden steepening of the *fjells,* a changing from slopes to craggy walls, so that as we turned back in our saddles in the defile of the Bövra we saw for the last time the rolling Dovre, Norway's ancient heart, as through the lintels of a door. When we turned again and rode, it was towards old, scarred mountains whose heads had whitened while the Alps still kicked in their cradles.

Man had come here too late to make history. "It was entirely unknown until the beginning of the last century . . . because of its wildness and secluded position, so entirely apart from all human habitation, it has been very difficult to explore until comparatively recent years." [1] The people of the Dovre had looked up fearfully at the towering parapets and bastions, the machicolated ramparts, and bent once more to the familiar soil. "This must be where the giants live," they said, "in the heart of this brooding forest." At night they gathered round the great fireplaces and told again the old sagas of the ogres with long, lank hair, gaping teeth, and maniacal features, who reared up from the *fjells* and reached down hands like tidal waves to sweep up human beings as a boy scoops up frog-spawn in his net. They are no mere over-grown men, no gawky Goliaths, these Nordic giants. It would have taken more than these to frighten the old Norse-men; they would have gone out with their broad swords and, if they could reach no higher, would have felled them as they fell the towering fir trees, and gone home with the scooped-out skulls as stew-pots for their prodigious meals. (The use of skulls as utensils seems to have been a habit of the early Norsemen; the ancient drinking-toast *"skaal"* still used today is from the old Norse word for skull.) A giant to be worth the telling must make the hearer shudder and his terror must exceed the courage of the audience. So these Nordic giants are as monstrous as mountains. One of the Edda mythologies, the Ragnarök, tells of the rising of the giants against the gods and men at the end of the world. A terrible winter is to come,

[1] Cook's *Scandinavia*.

lasting for several years, and at its end the giants and the monsters, the Thursar, are to rise against the gods.

> . . . *There crows*
> *A dusk-red cock in the halls of Hell,*
> *Wildly the hell-wolf howls from its lair,*
> *Breaks its chain and runs unchecked.*
> *Jotunheim roars! The Gods hold council of war.*

Thor and Odin lead the gods and the heroes of Valhalla against the giants and the Thursar. All fight to the death, leaving only the Thursar Surt, the death-flame or fire-wind, who stalks unhindered across the earth, burning to ashes all living things.

> *The Sun darkens, the earth sinks into the sea,*
> *The bright stars drop from the sky,*
> *The fire-wind withers the fertile trees,*
> *And flames lick up at Heaven itself.*

This, if one assumes as metaphors the long winter as the cold war, the gods as democracy, the giants as totalitarianism, and the death-flame or fire-wind as the nuclear bomb, gives a very good prophecy of the future as sometimes predicted today.

The road along the southern bank was still in the making and worsened as we went, becoming a mere levelled-out foundation of broken rocks. It was bad going for the horses, for their feet slipped and grated, so we dismounted and led them loose-reined that they might pick their steps. But there

was no way to either side: to the right the Bövra flowed deep
and quiet, to the left the crags rose high and steep. But at
last the road came to an end and we trod gratefully upon
God's good grass. So much of your pleasure depends upon
good going for the horses: when it becomes really bad you
must dismount and you are always worried lest the horses
sprain a tendon or come down on their knees. In country like
this it is easy to find yourself with a horse gone lame and
twenty miles to go to the nearest habitation.

The grassy track followed the river's narrow bank for four
or five miles till slowly it began to slant obliquely up the *fjell*
side and become stony. Soon it narrowed to a ledge that, seen
from the *fjells* across the close valley, would have seemed a
mere crack in the mountain wall. We dismounted again and
held the horses close up by the bits for better control, pushing
their heads towards the wall so that we might have foothold
on the track, for there was no room for horse and man to go
shoulder by shoulder in comfort and the river now seemed a
long way below.

There was a bad moment when we came to a couple of
deep steps formed by the strata of rock. Musti's off-hind foot
slipped, his shoe striking a sudden spark, and for an instant
he groped frantically upon the edge for a foothold. With a
lurch he heaved his leg back to the track and stood still,
snorting, till G.S. quieted him. But we had come to the
least practicable part of the track, and soon it improved,
eventually losing itself upon a steep and grassy hillside. A
few hundred feet below was our destination, a *bruk* marked

upon the map alongside the river. We slithered down and skirted a tilted field of potatoes, which Pilkis noted with approval, and rode into the farmyard. The farmer came from an outbuilding to stare at us, surprised that we came down from the mountain. Nor would we have done it, had we known that crazy goat track as he did.

It was a sparkling summer morning as we left the *bruk* over a sprightly beck and rode out upon a flat and grassy path beside the river. As we came round a bend in the valley, at its head there burst a white and shining vision into the sky—it was Glittertind, the "Glittering Peak," the poetry of its name exceeded only by its splendour scintillating in the vibrant blue of the sky. I believe that when God piled up a snow-clad mountain before such a sky He created the supreme beauty.

Soon we rode across a bridge over the river that carried away the opaque green meltings of glaciers lying upon the heart of the Jotunheimen, and came to the village of Böverdal, where we ate an early and unaccustomed lunch and discussed our route. In Lom we had heard that there was no village or farm beyond Böverdal till the far side of the Jotunheimen, forty miles ahead. If we tried to find our own way over the *fjells* there would be snow and perhaps bushes for the horses to eat and nothing for us. But there was a *fjellstue* at Bövertun some fourteen miles away, and here would be grass for the horses and good food for us. So we decided to go to Bövertun and from there over the Krossbu Pass, which becomes clear of snow about the middle of June.

The narrow road twisted magnificently up the valley, exposing at every turn new scenes of snow-clad *fjells,* and at last Galdhöpiggen, which beats its neighbour Glittertind by a few feet for the title of the highest mountain in northern Europe. But the morning had started too brilliantly to last; soon heavy clouds began to black out the sun, so that the world which had sparkled now dulled to a greyness of clouds and snow and rock which yet stressed the size and shape of the *fjells.* Where before they had been beautiful, now they were awful and tremendous. I who have always suffered gratefully from mountain mania was like a child at his first Western, twisting in my saddle as first Loftet, then Skagsnebb and grotesque Rundhöi displayed their chasms and chimneys, névés and arêtes in a serrated fantasia. For the first and last time on the journey I would as soon have gone on foot so that we could climb into the *fjells.* But soon we turned into a desolate valley of no great height or steepness and once more a horse became the best means of travel. Now the clouds dropped low and smothered the *fjells* and emptied a torrent of rain, so that in five minutes we were soaked to the skin and rode in sodden boots.

By the end of a long green-milk lake we came to the *fjell-stue* in a field of short mountain grass. Food was assured for all four travellers. After a meal we put up bootless feet to the luxury of a blazing log-fire in a fortunately empty room and watched with content the steam rising from our socks.

We saddled at dawn, for there was a long stage before us, beginning with a long, steady pull of a couple of thousand

feet up the Breidsaeterdalen. At first the walls of the valley
shut out the distant view, but at its top they opened to a far-
reaching panorama of *fjells* and snow and glaciers. To the
left the Smörstabb glacier spread out, seamed and wrinkled
and pierced by aiguilles like monstrous black teeth in a monstrous jaw; to the right climbed the last hundred feet of the
pass. Here snow combined with altitude to lower the temperature, for this is the highest pass in southern Scandinavia.
From its summit spread out a snowfield studded with rocks,
its far horizon broken by phallic peaks. It was a spiky, lunar
landscape of snow and rocks and crater-like tarns. You felt
that some space-ship, flying saucer, or similar fashionable
gadget might be resting here. But, thank God, folk-lore alone
and not science seemed interested in the Home of the
Giants.

It was a stirring day marred by misfortune. Musti began
to go halt on his near fore-leg; there was a puffiness around
the pastern suggestive of a sprain, so G.S. dismounted and
led him. The cause we did not know, though we suspected
the rough *fjell* track of two days before.

Later that evening we crept down tortuous hairpins to the
fjellstue of Turtagrö beneath the spires of the Hurrangane.
We bound Musti's leg with cold-water bandages that had
once been the top of my pyjamas; it was a poor night for
him, as food was scarce for the horses. But tomorrow they
would eat in the plenty of a fiord valley and then, too, they
would have left the snow for the last time—in July.

From Turtagrö there was a good track most of the way

down to Fortun at fiord level, but we thought the smoother surface of the road to be better for Musti's leg. Once more the way went steeply down for some five or six miles now hemmed by firs. Then the road came to what appeared to be a sheer drop, as though it was about to throw itself into space. We paused at the edge to look down for the last time from the Jotunheimen, between light and languid clouds to a flat and fertile valley dotted here and there by red farm buildings and lined with marshalled racks of hay, an instant change from wild mountains to cultivation and domesticity.

The road turned sharply left and coiled fantastically down a series of loops till at length and abruptly it came out on the flat floor of the valley, so that one minute you are coming down a crooked mountain road and the next you are strolling along a country lane among fields and hedges and homely cottages. There was a little café with tables and chairs upon a lawn, and everything was warm and sunny and green beneath the outer bastions of the Home of the Giants.

20. Fiords

He who wishes to travel far spares his steed. PROVERB

WE went from Fortun by the shore of a beautiful lake fed by the glaciers and reflecting upon the polished jade of its green, opaque surface a waterfall crawling upward to meet its twin that slid down the *fjell*. Soon we came to Skjolden, at the head of the Luster fiord. Musti's leg was still bad: he needed rest. To avoid holding up our progress G.S. suggested that he take Musti by fiord steamer to Kaupanger, where in any case we must take ferry across the Sogne fiord to Gud-vangen, while I rode on to meet him at Kaupanger. We went to the ship office on the jetty to inquire of its possibility: yes, there was a ship calling about six in the morning; it could take Musti in the hold by slinging him on board.

Next morning as we led Musti carefully from the stable the early stillness was startled by a hollow hoot that rolled around the *fjell* sides; upon the fiord a black speck was rest-ing like a fly upon a show-case, its only apparent movement a pair of white feelers twitching beneath its head. Musti limped gallantly along the road towards the jetty, his hoofs ringing through the sleeping village.

At last the ship drew in smartly but unconcernedly. No one seemed to be doing very much, but everything was done; the ship appeared to do her own changing of course and speed and judging of currents and tying-up, as though she had done so much of it that her crew left it to her. Certainly they did not seem to be anywhere about. Perhaps these Norwegian ships do not have crews; I never heard them, though occasionally I have seen a man in a sweater come up from below and light a pipe and stuff his hands in his pockets and breathe in a little salt air.

So it was that without warning a ship's crane let down a horse-sling, a square yard of strong canvas attached to ropes at each corner. It was slipped under Musti's belly by someone who had not been there a moment before; Musti let out a vicious, protesting kick, just missing the stranger, who seemed not to notice it, and the crane decided to swing him into mid-air and hang him over the open hatch. His legs kicked futilely, pitiful in their helpless power, and for a moment hoofs and head dangled like those of a cloth horse in a pageant. I hurried on deck and as he was lowered, slowly gyrating, I pushed his head away from the hatch sides; below, G.S.'s head was tilted tensely back to judge the landing, and as Musti came within a foot of the floor of the hold he grabbed the halter and steadied him. There was a sudden scuffle of hoofs as Musti's legs felt ground once more; then he went quietly to his stall.

A few minutes later the ship decided to move on; there was a beating and a frothing from her stern and she swung round and floated off down the fiord again, an empty ship but for a wave from G.S.'s arm.

I went back through the wakening street, wondering if St. Hubert, after seeing us through the snow and the forests and the marshes, through all the vicissitudes of climate and contour, had now gone back over the Jotunheimen and to the North till the next traveller should need him, and whether the troubles that could so easily have come upon us fatally in inconvenient places would now be with us. I felt he might have seen his way to stay a little longer.

Pilkis and I went from Skjolden about noon down the Luster fiord, feeling once more the temporary and decreasing pleasure of being alone. It is restful to travel alone for a change, with no one to interrupt the flow of your thoughts and your communion with Nature, but you can at last have enough of your own company. And soon now we should have to go each upon his own way: G.S. to Kristiansand to cross to Denmark, myself to Haugesund and so to England.

I feared a plague of tourist cars, but this proved groundless, for the Luster fiord is not one of the advertised ones. A warm day, a calm fiord where every *fjell,* beck, and tree was mirrored standing on its head, and the soothing enervation of coming down to sea level did not lead to hurry. It was scarcely mid-afternoon and we had gone no more than eight miles, and that leisurely, when we came to a little village. It was gathered in a bay that held its arms not close but folded back to display the *fjells* across the fiord. It had no hotel, no garage, no motor cars. It had a *pensjonat*,[1] a wooden quay, orchards of plum and cherry and pear, and a fourteenth-century church recalling that of Grasmere. The post office shared with the store an old wooden building upon the quay against which were fastened a couple of row-boats shaped like Viking long-ships, their gunwales rising to sharp stem and stern, a type still to be seen among the fiords. There was not a breath of bustle anywhere. I must stay here.

The white wooden *pensjonat* looked attractive. Its half-glazed and lace-curtained balcony stood on stilts halfway out over the road, giving it a southern European appearance. It looked clean enough to be pleasant, not so aseptic as to be soulless. A woman was standing upon the balcony; I rode up to her and said: *"God dag,"* then feeling instinctively that she spoke English: "Can you tell me if I can find a stable for my horse here?" She thought for a moment and said: "Well, I don't know really, I'll ask," and disappeared into the house.

It was difficult to place her. She was about middle age, with blond hair, and spoke English in what seemed at the time an affected accent, with no trace of guttural Scandinavian. She was probably from London and might have been an actress or music-hall artist when she was younger. Soon she came back with a Norwegian lad and said: "Jan will show you the way to a stable just down the road. What a lovely horse! What do you call her?"

Pilkis watered and fed, I went back to the *pensjonat*. My

[1] Pension.

new acquaintance was still on the balcony; I asked her whether there was a vacant room. *Pensjonats* are usually good places, cheap, with good food and friendly. She said yes, she thought so and would I come in—and made all arrangements for me while I wondered at the ease of her Norwegian. She spoke again of Pilkis, how she liked horses, and I remarked that all the way from Lapland we had seen only one ridden horse. She replied: "Of course; our country is very mountainous and is not good for riding."

"Oh," I said, "you've lived here for a long time?"

She smiled. "Yes, I am Norwegian-born. I'm up here with my husband; he's a painter. He loves this fiord; at the moment he's painting a picture of the church. Perhaps you have heard of him—Alf Lundeby?"

I admitted I hadn't. Later I found that he is one of the best-known Norwegian painters, dividing his time between the feminine colours of Italy and the rugged outlines of Norway. "But I thought you were English," I said. "You haven't any Norwegian accent."

"Haven't I? Well, you see, I was at Oxford for four years; perhaps that is why."

I felt my judgment had been poor. The grafting of the smooth Oxford speech had softened her Norwegian, and her nationality explained the fairness of hair, which stays blond in Scandinavian women without the use of bleaches.

Herr Lundeby and his wife were charming, intelligent, and kindly. Physically he is Shavian in his eighty years and white beard and the straightness of his back that would shame many a man of thirty. He invited me into the little church. A peeling of the tenth-century plaster had revealed murals of the seventeenth, and beneath these had been found paintings, on the original wall, that artists had declared to be of unusual quality and historical interest. So the complete wall was being carefully chiselled down to the original, a task expected to take three years. But time is nothing to Luster.

I left Luster with regret. But from the beginning G.S. and I had determined that there should be no tarrying except to rest the horses or from other necessity, and now I had to meet him again at Kaupanger. Had we dallied by every lotus plant, we should still be on our way. Once or twice towards the end of the ride we heard the singing of sirens, and though we are not indifferent towards them (on the contrary, we like 'em), yet, like Ulysses, we feared for our journey. So mentally we bound ourselves to the saddle, going regretfully but self-righteously on our way. At the head of a small fiord that branched off at right angles from the Luster fiord was a place marked on the map as Gaupne; this should be a convenient stopping-place for the night.

The road still clung to the steep *fjell* sides and for the last three miles became a mere ledge cut in the cliffs. There was no soft going here such as can usually be found on Norwegian roads, but a surface of unyielding rock where Pilkis's shoes rang out as though on metal. Gaupne was dismally prosaic after Luster; the road ran through it straight and flat for a mile between new and wire-fenced houses and a couple of stores. I left early and crossed the river at the head of the fiord by a long iron bridge and rode towards Marifjora on the far side of the fiord. The day was sunny and warm and this was a tranquil village with wooden jetties and rambling street bewitched by blowing blossom from the orchards. I left Pilkis on a patch of clover before a little store while I went inside. A white-haired old man was chatting amiably with a large and shaggy dog. They welcomed the arrival of a crony, and we talked together till at last I bought a packet of tobacco and went out upon my way.

From Marifjora the road wriggled for mile after mile up a long green valley speckled with farm-houses till it came out straight and breathless by a long and barren lake. By the far end of the lake it swooped downward hand-in-hand with a turgid river, ever deeper into a gorge, at last swinging away as the torrent suddenly toppled over a cliff into the narrow greenness of a valley five hundred feet below. There a homestead farmed the fertile strip by the now untroubled river. When later I looked back from the still steeply dropping road, there was the canyon's deep black mouth disgorging a massive pillar of water.

Very soon there came the calm Sogndalsfjord, curving narrow and almost land-locked. Today we had gone twenty miles, so we took our time upon the last four miles to Sogndal, stopping upon grassy patches for Pilkis's benefit or by clumps of wild raspberry bushes for mine. These raspberries, which grow much along the roadside in the fiord country, cheered many a lunchless day, for though the missing of morning and evening meals was now unusual we still often found ourselves away from food during the day.

I did not wish to stop in Sogndal but in its little offshoot across the fiord. We had to cross by ferry and I felt doubtful of Pilkis's attitude to ferry-travelling without the assurance of Musti's company, though the distance was less than half a mile. The ferry was of the flat, rectangular type guided by cables and driven by a small petrol motor housed in a cabin at one side, so that it had something of the form of a miniature aircraft-carrier. A car and a lorry boarded, followed by half a dozen local people and hikers bent beneath rucksacks. Pilkis led on easily enough; I unsaddled her at once and took out her bit, leaving only her halter. I did not expect serious trouble, but, should she take fright and break from me and jump into the fiord, she must not be hampered in swimming to the bank. On the starting of the motor she became restive, and I was thankful for the lorry in front of her and at last for the nudge that told of our landing. As I led her off she scampered across the ramp, but soon put her head down to graze in charge of a small boy while I went back for saddle and bridle. That evening she ate clover and grass, circling on her picket rope in a field now turned rich in colour by the dusk and sloping to the quiet depths of the fiord. Lights reached out from Sogndal across the placid water; everywhere was silence broken only now and then by the slow, hollow chug of the ferry taking its last leisurely evening strolls.

In the old farm-house where I stayed, there was a ladder

from the ground floor to the sleeping-quarters instead of a staircase so that it could be pulled up at night, no doubt a useful precaution in bygone days. My remarking on it brought a smile to the farmer's face; he told me of a house in the neighbourhood which perched upon a ledge above the fiord; there, he said, the only approach was by a rope ladder from the fiord, and not so long ago it used to be pulled up on the approach of tax-collectors.

We came next afternoon into Kaupanger. I led Pilkis to the post office, peering in from the end of her reins to ask the post-girl where I might find the Dane with the horse. "Oh, he's at Amla, a mile from here at the far side of the bay. You'll probably find him swimming." I went through the village smiling at the local knowledge of G.S., his habits, and their times. As we rode along the stony lane a hail came up from the sea: "Hi, Polar Rider! Where are you going?" And G.S. broke surface, a wet and whiskered walrus: I who swim like a windmill envied his long and easy movements. I rode Pilkis into the sea, where she kicked the water in delight.

G.S. had got himself a tent and encamped by a stable. This was typical of the eccentricity of our journey: in the North and the cold and the snow a lean-to groundsheet bivouac would do; now in the summer he must have a tent.

Musti had improved but little and was still unfit for riding, let alone going long distances. From Kaupanger we must in any case take ferry across the Sogne fiord to Gudvangen; we decided to go next day, and hoped that Musti would then be able to go short distances. We sat by the tent above the bay,

G.S. in his trunks upon a box, for the moment no longer a horseman but a beachcomber, cobbling his socks with painful diligence. My socks were never mended but, sordid skeletons, clung precariously to my feet: in this respect, as in many others, G.S. was the better traveller.

21. Horses' Ferry

The lame goes as far as the staggerer. PROVERB

MUSTI'S leg put a brake upon the half-mile walk to the ferry. As we went carefully down the slope to the quay, heads curious or impatient popped from the windows of tourist cars; but the horses strolled past this mechanical and so plebeian presence with fitting dignity. It seemed that they were to be tethered for'ard and so had to go on board before the cars; once they were secured, the cars moved in and took up their positions in well-ordered lines.

Soon the passengers gathered round the horses. Musti discouraged the over-curious with puckish nips unless they bribed him with titbits, thereby weeding out the worthless and leaving standing-room for honest men. At first the horses enjoyed the display put on for their benefit, till, tiring both of types and titbits, they turned rudely decisive rumps upon both and their capable mouths to life's essential—hay.

We went onto the upper deck to see the march-past of the

Sogne fiord, but it was shrouded in mist. In disappointment I tried out my improving Norwegian on a bulging brunette, who replied apologetically: "I'm sorry, I don't understand"— in an accent that came not far from Aberdeen. She looked forlornly for the *fjells* that could not be seen for the mist and remarked that it was just like home.

But the mist was clearing as the ferry came quietly to the runway at Gudvangen. The gangway settled down and poured out cars upon the road to speed away along the valley.

There did not seem much of interest in Gudvangen itself— a couple of hotels, three neat little shops, and perhaps a dozen houses; it seemed little more than a ferry terminal in the route linking the Sogne and Hardanger fiords, yet it is superbly set between the towering walls of the Näroydal, their grey crags decorated here and there by the tinsel of narrow waterfalls of such height that they seemed to settle down rather than drop.

Musti was obviously unfit for riding or even for leading more than short distances. It was decided that G.S. would come on slowly with Musti while I went on ahead to Eidfjord, which I particularly wished to see but which was unfortunately a day's ride to the east from our route; we should rejoin at Odde on the south side of the Hardanger fiord.

We walked in steady rain along the Näroydal till we came to a farm cramped between the walls: here G.S. stayed while I rode on to Stalheim some half-dozen miles further on. The tourist hotel stood up blatantly beside the pass at the head of the valley, but became more attractive as I approached, for it offered a chance to dry out clothes during the night while I slept in a bed.

So when Pilkis and I had climbed the hairpin bends and found that there was no farm here apart from the one belonging to the hotel, I was willingly forced to seek lodging in the hotel. I tied Pilkis to a tree before the doors and went in to the reception desk. "Could I have a stable for my horse and stay the night?" I could: the stable was now used for storing farm implements, but a stall could soon be cleared and I might have hay and oats from the farm.

The dinner was excellent but somewhat spoiled for me both by a niggling of the conscience that G.S. was probably not doing so well, and the staring of the guests. In Trondheim this curiosity had gone over our heads, but here I missed the moral support of another as odd as myself. But my self-consciousness was driven out by the interest of finding in the lounge some paintings by Lundeby—strong and rugged Norwegian landscapes in colours that we had often seen: strong greens and blues splashed with red, the colours of mountain ash against a summer sky. And later the strangeness of snowy sheets, h. and c., and a superfluous wardrobe was offset by the heartening sight of my clothes giving up their dampness from the warmth of a radiator.

In the morning clouds still sprawled across the *fjells,* oozing steady rain. As I lounged in the hotel, hoping for some clearing of the weather, a couple of buses swept round to the door and stopped to set free a gaggle of tourists, who flocked

into the lounge and its little curio shop. Soon it was tight
with joyous, exclaiming souvenir-hunters. Lapp curios were
wonderment: "Oh, just look at this little Eskimo! Isn't he
cute?"—indicated by the arm of a shapely sweater around the
bust of which lively reindeer chased unendingly. The cloth
figure of a Lapp regarded her stolidly from a show-case. Another visitor, short and fat and permed, came rapturously
from the counter swathed in a gay Lappish tunic and hat to
be admired by a friend. "Oh, Loretta, won't they be thrilled
back home?" And behind the counter the blonde girl helped
every whim with grave politeness and perfect English.

But the brightness inside did not spread beyond the doors.
Still all was grey above, and the steep *fjells* walling in the
Näroydal below glowered at each other like guards across a
hostile frontier. Either I spend the day in the Stalheim lounge
or get wet again. I decided on the latter. After pausing for
a moment to photograph the superb Näroydal, juggling with
exposures and apertures and filters in what proved a vain
hope of a good picture, we set off from the sweeping Hardanger road, Pilkis tucking in her head against the rain, myself
measuring time by increasing wetness.

We found quarters that night in a disused and dismal
stable. I bought some oats and a pile of hay from a farmer,
enough to pile Pilkis's manger and cover the floor of her
narrow stall that night and leave her a good breakfast for the
morning. Just as I borrowed her saddle-blanket to go over
me, so I borrowed her breakfast to go underneath, for the

stone slab that I was to sleep on seemed more than usually hard and cold. Soaking clothes are no flatterers of even the best of beds. I gave Pilkis a rubbing down and a strapping to dry and warm her. Outside it still poured. Having nothing better to do, I pulled out my diary, which was rarely written in—entries had become fewer and shorter ever since Kautokeino. Today was the first of August; also it seemed it was Lammas and Scottish Quarter Day. I had an idea that Lammas was a kind of harvest festival, a celebration of plenty: Scottish Quarter Day, I presumed, was a day for paying the house rent. A moment's thought suggested that neither concerned me very much; so, lacking inspiration, I wrote: "Soaking night. Stable stinks," stuffed a wet diary into wetter pocket, piled more hay in Pilkis's manger, took off my boots and stuffed them with hay to draw out the damp, pulled the blanket over me, and slept as peacefully as any man has ever done.

In the morning the farmer invited me to breakfast, so horse and man started in good spirits despite the continuing rain. But that evening Pilkis came into Voss with sore feet, placing them carefully before her, for once unwilling. Lately she had gone too much on unaccustomed roads and now needed rest on grass. So I resigned myself to missing Eidfjord after all and to two days in an uninteresting town set among undistinguished hills. Most of the time I slept while Pilkis ate rich grass and clover till her skin stretched tight as a tick's.

We left Voss, as it turned out, only a few hours before G.S. came in with Musti. The road clung to the electrified railway line that goes to Eide, but soon there was a track that led over the *fjells* and, moreover, cut off a corner. We followed its straying among the trees, at last coming out at a place that the map showed as Flatlandsmo. As expected, this was a single farm. From its unpainted house came an old man on sticks; the first impression was of age and lameness, but when he came near it was of brave blue eyes shining from a face wrinkled by weather and kindness, and of the straight slimness of his body. Then you no longer thought of him as either old or a cripple, for a man is these only when he gives way to them.

His one-stall stable bulged with the buttocks of his *fjording* mare, but Pilkis was welcomed to the barn. It was yet early afternoon, so I went out in the fields and helped his son with the haymaking. The family name was also Flatlandsmo, giving its name to the place, as often is the case in Norway. Such people are the true aristocrats in a country that has no titles.

From Flatlandsmo the road continued by the railway as far as the wide-swinging hairpins of Skervet, which were pierced by the Skervetfoss and dropped down a thousand feet to a tight little valley that at last widened out to the placid Granvinvatn. Though Pilkis was much better, she was not yet her usual self, so I decided to do only a short stage to the village of Granvin. Here I stayed with a farmer and helped him with his hay, seeing something of the working of a Norwegian *fjell* farm.

Few things breed good common sense and ingenuity more

than living where Nature is awkward. Only twenty per cent
of Norway is below the five-hundred-feet line, and a good
deal of this is rock. Due to its northerly latitude, the snow-
line is much lower than in the Alps or the Pyrenees, so that
most of the country is under snow in the winter. Thick forests cover much of even the low-lying land. Many farms and
some villages are approachable only by sea or mountain
tracks. On the face of it, an impossible country for a farmer.

When he takes over *fjell* land to make his farm, he fells
the timber on the flattest area and with it builds his house, his
outbuildings, and his fences. Then he clears any flat patches
on the *fjell* side and sows grass, and when this grass is cut he
drapes it over wires slung between posts. One good drying-
day and, like a housewife's washing, it is ready to take in. But
there is no loading into a waggon, carting, and throwing up
into a barn, with all the need of extra labour. He puts up a
hay-lift—rather like a ski-lift, but with traffic moving down
instead of up. A wire cable is run from the barn up to the
most convenient patch, and rigged up on wooden trestles
some ten or twelve feet high like train wires from their posts
—and there he has an overhead railway line worked by grav-
ity, the cheapest of all power. A dozen or so pulleys with
hooks and some lengths of rope are now all he needs. The
hay is taken from the racks, laid lengthwise across a rope, the
rope tightened and fastened and hung on a pulley, and away
it all goes, hell-for-leather, sixty miles an hour down between
the pines till it sweeps into the barn and leaps the wire—and

there is the hay, carted and thrown in the barn above the stable. In the winter when the snow is deep upon the ground, he cuts timber for his fire and drops it also down to his barn by the cableway.

Just as he uses the steepness of the land outside, so he does inside the stable. His stable is built on the slope, its door toward the *fjell,* its back towards the valley. Beneath the stable floor is the midden. In the gutter behind the animals are holes about a foot square, filled in by thick wooden trapdoors. When the stable is mucked-out, the doors are lifted, the dung swept down the holes, the doors put back—and the stable is clean once more. There are no drains to block, no wasted urine, no waste of fertility by the washing of rain, and no wasted labour by shovelling the dung into a wheelbarrow and trundling it outside. So instead of being bullied by his mountain, the farmer makes it work for him.

A quiet ride along the shore brought us to Eide, yet another fiord village with its little post office on the quay. G.S. came in by evening; Musti and Pilkis joined once more with neighing and nudging and nosing.

The manager of the hotel asked us if we would care to give a talk to an English party that was staying there. We were not keen, but it seemed that we had done a lot of taking in Norway and little giving, so we lied that we should be pleased. We took the tattered map from a saddle-bag, rubbed up our boots with straw and straightened our clothes with incongruous precision. The map was pinned upon a door as a valuable ally to a connected account. When one showed signs of drying up, the other stepped in, so that the talk never faltered in spite of lack of preparation and our amateur status.

In the morning a tail of children fastened to us as we went to the jetty, as though we were a pair of Pied Pipers.

The embarking of the horses was a tricky business that came near to disaster. The little ship was held away from the quay by wooden floats; there was no wide ramp onto it as there had been onto the ferry at Kaupanger, nor was there a sling such as the one that had embarked Musti at Skjolden. The only way on board was by passenger gangway. Musti was led to it first; he saw the gap below and refused. I tried Pilkis, but with no more success. Every trick was used from backing to blindfolding, but they had seen the drop to the fiord and the moment their hoofs touched the gangway they stopped and set themselves. Someone brought straw to lay on the gangway and deaden the hollow sound of their hoofs, but they were not to be fooled. At last we borrowed another gangway and fastened them side by side, detaching the two centre rails. I led Pilkis to them, and again she refused, but at the second attempt she decided that this new broad path was perhaps not too bad, and ventured it. Halfway up, her old fear returned and she lost her nerve, her hoofs slipping and drumming as she pushed me against the rail. A hind leg slipped over the side. A woman screamed. I flung myself at Pilkis's shoulder; it steadied her, and she lurched her foot back onto the gangway and leaped onto the deck. With a shaking hand I calmed her, while I watched Musti placidly following G.S. on board.

There was no accommodation for horses on the little ship such as there had been on the car ferry to Gudvangen, so, as it was raining, they occupied a deep bed of hay on a deck passage-way, Pilkis's nose inquiring at the pantry, Musti's hams turned disrespectfully against the second engineer's cabin. In Norway kindness is usually greater than propriety: no one seemed to be disturbed; you felt that horses came regularly to the pantry door and that the second engineer often opened his door upon the rump of a horse.

At Odde we saw the first sign of industry in Norway. A grid of four monstrous pipes sprawled from top to bottom of the *fjell* side, containing a once-beautiful waterfall; from the centre of the small town a chimney erupted smoke and stench that drifted down, yellow and acrid, upon a modern Pompeii.

Next day was a depressing one. Tomorrow we should go our respective ways; Musti's leg was little better and he had still to be led; this was the eleventh day of rain, soaking our clothes that had half dried out during the night. As the North has probably cured me for ever of complaining of the cold, so the south of Norway may cure me of any heart-felt grumble about rain. Neither Wales nor the Lake District has ever soaked me so continually. People nodded thoughtfully and said: "There's not been a summer like this for fifty years. Weather isn't what it used to be." No doubt they were right. It never was.

We went along a close but unimpressive valley, relieved only by the Latefoss, which drops several hundred feet down the *fjell* side and surges beneath a many-arched bridge, as through the sluice-gates of a dam. Fittingly, we found quarters that night in a draughty barn.

22. The Ways Divide

Horses he loved, and laughter, and the sun,
A song, wide spaces and the open air;
The trust of all dumb living things he won,
And never knew the luck too good to share:
Now, though he will not ride with us again,
His merry spirit seems our comrade yet. . . .
LINES IN *Punch* AFTER THE BATTLE OF MESSINES

OUR parting was a genuine farewell. There was nothing said unmeant, no conventional politenesses. Merely we shook hands firmly and said: "Well, cheerio, and good luck," and turned to our horses, mounted, and rode upon our ways. As Pilkis, returning Musti's neighs, climbed the mountain road to Haugesund, I twice turned in the saddle and searched the pines below for a white ribbon threading the green valley and found there a crawling speck, a man and his horse. I waved high for recognition; from the speck uncoiled a minute tentacle like a fly's leg, slowly circling.

At last the road topped a ridge and dropped to a tortuous valley. On its brow I turned Pilkis to a halt against the skyline; a last movement of the speck below answered my up-held arm. Then we turned and went, saddened in spite of a welcome sun, down to the defile before us. Pilkis seemed to sense the finality of this farewell and went slowly with droop-ing head, wondering perhaps at the selfishness of men that they separate good friends at their convenience.

All day we went in the sun through gorges of hot black rock that threw down its heat upon us. For the first and last time on the journey it was unpleasantly warm, so we were glad to come down at last towards the fiord at Fjaera and feel its evening coolness blowing up to us. Here in Fjaera Pilkis ate and slept in a stable now occupied by hens hunched upon their perch, blinking broodily down at the strange visitor, while I slept, an invited guest, in a kind, primitive little *pensjonat*.

The floor of the ravine down which we came goes head-long through Fjaera and dives beneath the encroaching fiord; the Haugesund road just in time swings to the left across a short iron bridge and goes clinging desperately along the wall that springs a couple of thousand feet from the grey coldness of the fiord. How far down is its floor possibly no one could tell you, but they can say that a liner would sink there without trace. The fiords, having been scooped out in the glacial age, are perhaps a million years younger than the peaks of Jotunheim and Kiolen, so there has been little time for erosion to fill their bottoms or slant their near-perpendicu-lar walls. Thus, they are often deeper than the ocean around the coasts.

The road in the first ten miles of its way to Kyrping bores through twelve tunnels and leaps across twelve bridges like a gigantic version of a scenic railway on a fairground. Pilkis pricked suspicious ears at the first of these tunnels, and inside it the hollow echoes of her hoofs disturbed her; but when she found there was no harm she treated the rest with indifference as though she had spent half her life walking in and out of black tunnels with an ever growing target of light that suddenly grew big and became the wide, free world. But in all I kept watch for vehicles so I might dismount and wave a warning handkerchief in their headlights.

Beyond the last tunnel and bridge the *fjells* finally gave place to hills. We halted that I might look back upon their friendly grandeur where we had travelled happily and which we now sadly left. I wondered whether anywhere in the world could be seen more variety of Nature than from this patch of grass stippled with yellow flowers. To the left and below us a river rambled through a fertile valley; before us the deep fiord, widening to the sea in the west, reached across to the piled *fjells* that culminated in mighty Folgefonna with its head covered by a vast glacier like white and soaking locks of hair that drained in slender waterfalls upon its face; to the right the forest spread upwards over the *fjell* sides. Soon gathering clouds warned us to be on our way, and we rode down to Kyrping, which browsed in the gentle valley.

From Kyrping the journey's finale began. It lasted six days, but might easily have been done in four; our journey had been delightful, and now that its end was near I hung on to it nostalgically. The country, reminiscent of the west coast of Scotland, seemed mild by comparison with the stupendous hinterland behind us. But it was all very pleasant: there was the shapely Stordalsvatn, its shores and hills all feminine curves; the calm little tongue of fiord at Etne, into which I took Pilkis for the good of her legs and the pleasure of my nose; the track from Etne to Olen, which had once been the road before the time of motor cars and now wandered in delicious privacy by inlets and woods and wild-flower scents; Olen, last of the fiord villages of quaint wooden buildings and jetties and fish-curers and sea-smells and calling ships that dwarfed everything; and the pleasant walk over the hills from Olen to Skjold with a young Englishman who had been hiking on the Hardanger plateau, while Pilkis trailed contentedly at heel like a dog.

As we approached Skjold, a young man came alongside on his bicycle and invited us to stay at his farm and stable Pilkis there. Even I who knew hospitality so well was surprised that anyone should come out to offer it, though this had happened once or twice before. In the evening his wife brought out her spinning-wheel as another woman would her knitting. She was amused by our interest (after all, what was so wonderful in a spinning-wheel?), but our only acquaintance with them had been in fairy stories and more recently in antique shops. To us it was as unusual, and therefore as fascinating, as a man in a suit of armour. She showed us how she carded the raw wool between wire brushes and spun it into thread upon her wheel to knit clothes that were warm, hard-wearing, and almost waterproof because the grease and the nature had been left in the wool.

At the next farm I was shown another kind of home industry. The farmer was fuddled; he spoke thickly and smelt like a distillery. After we had eaten, he asked in a cautious and confiding whisper if I would like a drink. He beckoned to me, and I followed him down a flight of steps to a cellar. He had the air of a kind of minor Guy Fawkes, but there seemed no reason why he should wish to blow up either his own house or a traveller so obviously a pauper; so, curious, I followed him. He shut the door behind us and crossed the cellar to another door hidden by a pile of crates. He opened it, shut it quietly behind us, and switched on a subdued light. There upon a wooden bench were the workings of an illicit still. Several large bottles filled with a dark liquid that looked like black treacle and with the necks stuffed with what seemed to be cotton wool, were inverted over beakers into which dripped a liquid as clear as spring-water. From curiosity and to avoid offence I took a sip from an offered mug. But only one. By comparison vodka, arak, or Cape brandy are soft drinks and Navy rum a soothing syrup: my throat felt as though it had been seized by a crocodile and had boiling oil poured down it for good measure. The farmer regarded my contortions with approval: obviously his was a good brew. In the morning my gullet was still raw as I mounted Pilkis for the last stage of a journey.

23. Unsaddle

How dull it is to pause, to make an end,
To rust unburnish'd, not to shine in use.
SHELLEY

JUST as our expectations for the start of the journey proved false, so did mine for its finish. Many times during the long stages, in the quiet hours when we rode apart, a shivering body and an empty stomach had been warmed and heartened by the thoughts of the moment when at last we should rein in and slide from the saddle and say: "Well, we've done it." The sun would smile down on us in approval, we should swim luxuriously in the summer sea and change into clean and less conspicuous clothes. There would be no more worry about finding shelter for the horses. Life would relax and laze for a while. Not one of these things happened. There was nothing inspiring under the sun, and no sun either. A drab sky drooled steady rain. A few ten-kroner notes insufficient for celebration clung together damply in my pocket. I had to go on wearing old clothes which, though ideal for the road, were conspicuously out of place in Haugesund. There was no peace: reporters with a scent to shame a ferret tracked down their prey (it seemed I was no longer a Polar Rider or a Riding Beard, but the Riding Briton). Above all, I was worried to know what to do with Pilkis, for, due to the stringency of veterinary regulations for import, I could not take her to England as I had hoped. She could have been sold to pull a cart in the streets, but this I did not wish. The satisfaction of success was less than the regret that we no longer travelled: truly "it is better to travel hopefully than to arrive."

Haugesund was the only Small Town that I came to in Norway: it was neither large enough for tolerance nor small enough for easy friendliness, nor was it old enough to be mellow. It dressed uniformly, lounge-suited and felt-hatted; it walked up and down its main street (those of lesser social status walked the less main streets) and looked at and gossiped about itself. Its streets ran straight, its public gardens were immaculate. Its concrete bridge is the largest in Norway.

Thus it is the sort of place where oddity is stared at. That is why I shaved. Or, rather, I hacked. A pallid patch of skin took the place of the Beard, contrasting with the weather-stain of months in a kind of skewbald effect. I had hoped I should pass a little less noticed. I didn't. Haugesund looked and said: "The Riding Briton has lost his beard. Just fancy, a Riding Briton without a beard! Come and see!" It served me right for ratting, for G.S. had gone to Denmark boldly bearded.

But I had three or four very good friends in Haugesund. I stayed with a young artist and his brother who had been interested in press reports of the ride and had offered hospitality as I rode into the town. The cheery editor of the *Haugesunds Dagblad* more than repaid me for the writing of an article by advertising Pilkis for sale. Just as helpful and friendly was Mr. Erikson of the tourist bureau, a linguist, a humorist, and a great character who knew everyone in the town and was quietly amused by most of them. He showed me the National Monument upon the cliffs north of the town; commemorating the first union of Norway under one king, the great Harald Fairhair, it stands upon his supposed grave. Around a central forty-foot-high obelisk, the Harald stone, are grouped smaller stones brought from each of the counties whose kings he subdued. A geologist might get a fair idea of the rock structure of Norway without stirring from Haugesund.

But one piece of publicity was welcome. I was asked to give a talk on the journey over the radio; this meant a pleasant trip of a few hours by sea to Stavanger.

Stavanger is a place with personality. The harbour strolls into town so that ships stand over the streets as do houses, for Norwegians like ships and so decorate their towns and villages with them. To a lover of ships this is fascinating, and in his satisfaction he nods in a friendly way from his window to a sailor upon his deck. The Viking still lives, if not now so picturesquely clad.

I went by taxi to the broadcasting-house, a mental laziness

to avoid a search rather than a dislike of walking. It was small by B.B.C. standards, but tasteful and intimate. And in the morning I woke to find a shining Atlantic liner standing monstrously above my window.

A few days later I sold Pilkis to an officer of the Norwegian army, Major Ording. The relief was great, for few horses are better treated than army horses: their food is uniformly good, they are under the care of vets, and the punishment for ill-treatment of a horse is rightly severe. In point of fact, troopers usually become much attached to their mounts: one of my memories that will last was the final parade of a famous cavalry regiment before it changed to armoured cars. At the dismissal there were more moist eyes than dry ones in the hard faces of hard men, and in the stable afterwards there was silence. To have kept its horses that regiment would have fought as it had never fought before in a splendid history. Then the vehicles arrived. The faces of the regiment twisted in contempt. After the first parade there was no silence this time, but a threatening rumble of oaths and abuse only sadly and half-heartedly rebuked by the officers. To "swear like a trooper" is no false attribute.

Major Ording was an Olympic rider and perhaps the best-known horseman in Norway, and I knew that a horse in his care would be well looked after. During the German occupation he worked for a fortnight as a white-aproned employee in a dry-cleaner's, pressing the clothes of soldiers who were searching for him in the *fjells,* before he slipped out beneath their noses in a fishing-boat and came to England. From time to time I hear from him to say that Pilkis is well, though, alas, I fear that military discipline does not permit her rolling on potatoes.

A letter came from G.S. from Denmark.

Arrived Kristiansand at 9 o'clock night yesterday. Boat left at 7 o'clock. Got Musti in a crate. Sea a bit unquiet—so Musti.

To-day arrived at 6 o'clock morning. First thing on Danish soil was Musti a roll and owner an ale. No trouble with the arriving vet. Musti's leg went very bad 10 miles from Kristiansand. He was so lame that he could hardly walk. I prayed that he would get better—I really did—and after five minutes grazing he was more gay and sounder than ever— and has been since. I couldn't tell you how he got better but it felt very strange as he was definitely constantly bad for some time before.

Now time is two o'clock. I am at the local inn with Musti in the garden. Must find him a farm now. I am resting here for 4 days. Big sandy beach for miles but no sun to-day. Heard on boat that you had been to Stavanger for broadcast. Good Show.

Must finish now.

Good luck old boy,

Yours

GORM

In England later I heard from him of the end of his ride. He had a triumphal entry into Copenhagen: a mounted police escort was sent out to meet him, crowds walled the streets, that night he and Musti appeared in the ring at the Copenhagen Circus. He was welcomed to the Adventurer's Club, he spoke on the radio, the press interviewed and photographed him till he was sick of them. One paper ranked his ride with the great journeys of Charles XII and Mannerheim.

Pilkis cared for, there was nothing to keep me here. A ship was leaving Bergen for England next day; I could catch it by going on the evening coastal ship from Haugesund. My friends came on board to see me off, and there was a farewell round of drinks taken secretly behind the bar, as the ship was in bond. For the last time I raised my glass to say: "*Skaal.*"

Ways of living die hard. It did not at the time seem out of place that I went on board at Bergen with my saddle and its wallets and sleeping-bag upon my arm as though from unsaddling Pilkis, nor that I still wore travel-stained boots and breeches. Perhaps this was because of thoughts of my good companions in experience—G.S. and the horses: horses who, tired and hungry though they often were, had never refused an obstacle. Theirs was the honour.

Rarely does anything remain along the route of a journey but memories and jetsam: as the ship quickened from the harbour I went to the stern rail and looked northward along the ragged coast till it dipped into the dusk. A thousand miles beyond was a great solitude of snow, and nearer a vast forest, in its midst the rotting legs of pyjamas hung there in foolish caprice; eight worn-out horseshoes, once necessary to a purpose, brought over the great Kiolen by two Northern horses and now rusting by a stable door; up in the snow that lies upon the *fjells* alien hoofmarks, as though of some Abominable Snowman; here and there a memory of two travellers who came unexpectedly by night and in the morning went away upon their strange journey; in lonely forests or high up in the *fjells* sodden circles of ash soaking back to earth, and from one of these patches in a silent marsh, a trail of gashes upon trees leading to a village; perhaps even yet, in the marshes, a withered scrap of paper with washed-out writing, flapping limply against a branch.

As night was now falling, two horses would be at rest, pulling at their hay, and munching . . . munching . . . munching.

Postscript

AFTER the manuscript had gone to the publishers, this appeared in a national newspaper:

SOVIET SPY RINGS IN NORWAY
SEVERAL ARRESTS
From our Correspondent
STOCKHOLM, FEBRUARY 8

The Norwegian police are breaking up a spy ring in Oslo which may turn out to have been one of the most dangerous organisations working for the Soviet Union in Scandinavia since the war. Several people have been arrested, among them Aasbjörn Sunde, who became notorious for his daring activities as chief of the Communist Resistance movement during the war. Only two months ago, in Northern Norway, another spy ring was broken up after it had been given away by a renegade Soviet officer.

The security service is reported to have been on the tracks of the Oslo ring for five years. Surveillance of its members has, however, been very difficult as the Russians have used the method of "snatching up" their Norwegian collaborators and their reports in cars at places previously agreed upon. It was on such an occasion, when he was about to hand over a report, that Sunde was seized. He was taken completely by surprise and offered no resistance. . . .

A number of serious spy cases involving Scandinavia has been unveiled during the past few years and are causing growing concern. In 1951 the so-called naval spy, Andersson, was sentenced to life imprisonment for betraying information of vital importance to Swedish defence. The following year a ring was broken up after having supplied the Russians with reports on the extremely important Swedish defence system along the Finnish frontier. At about the same time as the espionage in Northern Norway was detected last autumn a spy ring was caught also in Finland.

This may explain a lot. I am now reminded, too, of a Norwegian at Kautokeino who puzzled us by saying: "It would be better if you didn't continue this journey"; of two Swedes, bearded and dirty from travel in the *fjells,* who were the only other guests at the inn at Karesuando and who sat with us at meals. Their interest in our plans was perhaps too obviously casual, and when one mentioned "The Captain," G.S. noticed that the other rapped his shins under the table. And there was the strange visitor at Galanito. But is it all clear even yet? Espionage, as well as counter-espionage, is interested in those it suspects.

A NOTE ON THE TYPE

This book is set in Granjon, a type named in compliment to Robert Granjon, type-cutter and printer—Antwerp, Lyon, Rome, Paris—active from 1523 to 1590. The boldest and most original designer of his time, he was one of the first to practice the trade of type-founder apart from that of printer.

This type face was designed by George W. Jones, who based his drawings upon a type used by Claude Garamond (1510–61) in his beautiful French books, and more closely resembles Garamond's own than do any of the various modern types that bear his name.

The book was composed, printed, and bound by The Plimpton Press, Norwood, Massachusetts. Paper manufactured by S. D. Warren Company, Boston, Massachusetts.